The
Sea Sprite
Inn

Cat & Mouse Press
Lewes, DE 19958
www.catandmousepress.com

Dedication

He told me not to use his name, but without him, writing this novel would still be a dream. He believes in me and kicks my ass when I don't believe in myself. He worked through story lines and endless questions until the wee hours without ever rolling his eyes. And he did it because I was writing this book for you—a book that he would never, never-ever, in a million years, choose to read for himself.

Every day, after working fourteen hours, he came home and took care of us ... and the chores. He did it alone for months—while I was lost in the words. The most wonderful part of my day was him tapping softly on the wall between us, just to let me know how much I'm loved.

Thank you for finding me, loving me, keeping me. I love you more—even though I've been known to roll my eyes on occasion.

In Memoriam

Claudia Jo

June 1944–June 2015

To recap one of our last conversations:

"Promise me you'll finish the book. I can't wait to see how it ends."

"Mom—only you could guilt me into something, even after you're dead."

P.S. I hope you like the end. I miss you.

Acknowledgments

My thanks to Jennifer Weiner, who offers ten nuggets of advice for writers. So Jen, I rescued a dog—you know, #6 on your list. He sheds ... a lot. When I walk him, I think about writing. When I sweep my floors, I think of you. His name is Bueller (strictly for the fun of calling him), and he is also grateful for your advice.

To my friend Lyn Newsom—thank you for your dedication, support, and strained eyeballs. We were so enthralled with the process, we often forgot to eat until almost bedtime. Those late-night pizzas were well worth any additional dimples in my thighs. Without your tireless support, I would still be lost in the edits. Prepare yourself; I want to do it again.

Many thanks to Shirley Stout for beta reading during her convalescence. Thanks for being such a "captive" audience. This'll teach you not to break your ankle again.

I owe a huge load of thanks to Nancy Day Sakaduski of Cat & Mouse Press. Thanks for seeking out this enthusiastic first-time novelist and taking a chance. As both editor and publisher, your suggestions and patience thoughtfully guided me through the unfamiliar territory of writing a book. You switched a thousand puzzle pieces around, and because of your efforts and knowledge, I came through unscathed with a much better story.

Finally, to Beverly Cleary— thanks for helping me escape with Ramona, Beezus, Henry, and Ribsy.

PROLOGUE

ithout an end, Jillian thought, *there could be no beginning.* The Sea Sprite Inn was about to become a reality.

Brad's beat-up truck pulled in, honking its way up the length of the driveway. Jillian rushed out to meet him. He was a phenomenal contractor, but he never seemed to remember that her Rehoboth neighbors liked to sleep late. When Jillian saw the reason for his excitement, she couldn't chastise him. The workers lifted the sign from the truck and lugged it onto the porch. The crisp yellow cushions on her grandmother's black wicker chair welcomed her to sit and watch. Her next-door neighbor Barb—awakened by all the honking and too nosy to simply gaze out the window—joined Jillian on the porch. The men carefully removed the packaging.

"Well, what do you think?" asked Brad.

"It's perfect," was all Jillian could muster as she took in The Sea Sprite Inn sign. The playful sprite seemed to be sprinkling magical dust from her little wand, as if raining luck on the guests who would soon be coming through the front door. Barb nodded her head in agreement and reached over to give Jillian a hug.

Jillian was thankful she and Barb could share this special moment. Her neighbor was such a big supporter, always showing up at the right moment with a pot of hot tea or lemonade and cookies. In fact, they had come up with the name "The Sea Sprite Inn" during a tea-time chat. Jillian squeezed Barb tightly.

This was it. The finish line. The moment this beautiful sign was hung, her new journey would start. Unable to stop herself, the tears spilled over.

"OK, boys, let's get her up there. Careful now. Watch the end," Brad directed. Thirty minutes later, the sign was hung—cheerful and proud—over the porch.

The Sea Sprite Inn was open.

THE BEGINNING

*J*illian went to her grandfather's home early and alone. She could hardly believe it had been so long since she had last been here. Standing in the front yard, she absorbed the cockeyed, rotted shutter, disconnected from its window, drooping precariously and covering most of the panes. The columns on the verandah—once painted glossy white and as smooth as a pair of freshly shaved beach legs—now stood weather-pitted and weak, tired of holding up the porch roof. Above them, the jagged glass of a broken bedroom window hid in shame under a canopy of ivy. Fanciful gingerbread trim that used to evoke long-ago parties now mimicked the missing teeth in a seven-year-old's smile. Her lifelong best friend, Amy, had warned her Gramps' place was looking rough, but it had suffered much more than she expected. Jillian had suffered, too. Moving back into her childhood home had seemed like a good solution, especially since Gramps would need help when he got out of rehab.

The key felt cold in her hand. Standing on the familiar porch, surrounded by shedding paint that crunched under her shoes and the weight of her own failures, Jillian gave the key a solid push into the tarnished brass lock. She lifted the matching doorknob up and to the right—just as she remembered—and the door swung open, welcoming Jillian to her new world.

The gasp was involuntary. The sense of shame she felt when greeted by the disaster was overwhelming. It was worse inside. Much worse. Gone was the tidy interior that, in the past, enthusiastically invited everyone to cross the threshold. In fact, from where she stood, the place didn't even look habitable. She walked past the mounds of unopened mail spilling onto the floor of the foyer and entered the living room. Regret and a deep sorrow filled her heart.

Grabbing the closest corner of a dingy sheet flung over half of the sofa, she lifted her hand. Two fingers pierced the dry-rotted fabric, sending millions of tiny dust particles to dance on stale air. To encourage Jillian, sunlight lit them from above, creating an energetic light show. The house seemed to be begging her for attention.

Walking through the downstairs, Jillian realized that even if she worked as hard as she could for a month, it was only enough time to make a tiny dent in the disaster. She turned the water on full force in the kitchen sink and started scraping petrified food from the dishes. The counter was littered with open cans of half-eaten soup. Layers of oil remained in otherwise empty tuna fish cans, and there were two empty cases of beef jerky in the corner.

Pushing her sleeves above her elbows, Jillian lowered her hands into the full sink. *No hot water?* The faucet groaned in protest as she turned it off and headed to investigate the water heater. There was a clear, sharp knock at the front door. *Damn it, not now.*

Tufts of pink hair caught Jillian's eye as she made her way to answer. She opened the door to find a vibrantly colorful, skinny little toothpick of a woman covered in wrinkles, smiling at her.

"Hiya, doll! I'm Barb. Barbara McNally, from next door. Sorry to bother you, but I'm worried about Georgie." When Barb smiled, it took up half of her face, and her eyes hid behind the apples of her cheeks. "I try to keep my eye on him so he doesn't get in too much trouble."

"Oh. Thank you." Jillian stammered a bit, taken aback by this energetic whirlwind. "I'm Jillian, Georgie's ... umm ... George's granddaughter."

"He's told me all about you. Couldn't be prouder of you and your daughter. Brags about you all the time. Told me you're some kind of bigwig accountant for a law firm, right? So how is the old coot?"

"He took a fall and has a broken shoulder. And he may have suffered a stroke. He'll probably be in rehab for several weeks."

"I told him he wasn't drinking enough water. Think he'd listen to me? No. Most stubborn man I ever met. He eats all that salty stuff and doesn't drink. I told him it was turning his blood to glue. Well, at least I can say 'I told you so' next time I see him. I do love being right."

Jillian smiled. "Thanks for watching out for him. I wish he would've listened to you, too. But if you'll excuse me for now, Barb, I've got so much to do before. . . ."

"Say no more, doll. Happy to meet you. I'm sure I'll see you again." She spun off the verandah and marched toward her house.

⚷

No wonder Gramps always insisted on visiting me in Annapolis, she thought. *He certainly fooled me. Now, where do I go from here?* She picked up the phone and dialed her best friend. *Amy will know what to do.*

Jillian climbed the staircase and walked into her childhood bedroom. She opened a box labeled with her name scrawled in giant, black Sharpie letters. The last of the rotted tape peeled away, and Jillian was met with a barrage of memories she had guarded fiercely for years. Then she sat down on her old bed to wait for Amy.

Jillian was relieved when she heard the front door open and bang shut. Footsteps entered the foyer and stopped. She heard a low whistle.

"Holy hell in a handbasket." Amy whistled again. "Jilly! Where are you?" Amy pounded up the steps and found Jillian clutching an old Barbie, trying not to sink under the weight of it all. "OK, take a deep breath. It's all fixable. It's never as bad as it seems. It's not the end of the world. We'll get through it. We're gonna take it one step at a time. After all, you can't eat an elephant in one bite. Right?"

Jillian smiled weakly, in spite of herself. "Do you realize how many clichés you were able to cobble together in one breath? It's truly remarkable. What's even more surprising is, I so want to believe you."

"You'll see. I'm going to call Brad, my contractor. He'll give you a great price, and we'll get this place fixed up in no time."

❦

Jillian walked around her grandfather's house with a tablet of paper and a ballpoint pen. The list was so overwhelming, she didn't know where to begin. The sound of crunching gravel in the driveway announced the arrival of Amy and the contractor. Jillian went downstairs with her notes to greet them.

Amy jumped in headfirst. "Jilly, this is Brad. Brad, Jilly. I can't stay long, so I drove separately. Ready to give him the rundown?"

Brad looked the part. Faded, ripped jeans were held together with caulk, spackle, and splashes of every color of paint imaginable. His hair was ... well ... Jillian wasn't sure exactly what color it was because it was coated with white drywall dust. His eyebrows matched. He clomped around the foyer with heavy boots, and each step sent up a billow of dust. Two pens were perched behind his ear, and when he reached for one, Jillian was surprised to see that two of his fingers were missing. He caught her staring.

"Aww, that? It's nothing. Accident on the last project. But don't worry, their lawyers took good care of me." Jillian's eyes widened in fear. "Nah, I'm messing with you," he said with a laugh. "Happened when I was young."

"Oh, real funny, Brad," scolded Amy. "Let's get to work."

Jillian filled Brad in on the details of how she had inherited the responsibility for the old home and was trying to figure out what to do with it. So far, Brad remained silent. His three good fingers gripped the pen and started taking notes. In the living room alone, he filled up two pages. They passed through the foyer again and entered the dining room.

"These rooms are huge." Brad studied the ceilings and passed into the kitchen without taking any notes. "Hmmm." His scribbling resumed.

"You know, we aren't mind readers," said Amy.

"Well, there's a lot of space to work with." He turned and walked back to the dining room.

"Hmm," he said. "Huh." He crossed through the foyer to the living room.

After scratching his stubbled face, he took a quick breath as though he were going to speak, but then didn't. After the third round of the same actions, Amy shoved her fingers through her blonde hair and sighed. "For crying out loud. What are you thinking?"

He looked up and smiled crookedly. "Well, that could work," he said to no one in particular. Then he turned to both of them. "Why don't you turn this into one of those bed and breakfast places? Have a room down here and extra rooms upstairs to rent." For several moments, gears turned as the women digested his words.

It didn't take long for Amy to jump all over his suggestion. She squealed with excitement and ran to Jillian, grasping both of her shoulders. "That's *it*! There's the answer, Jilly. You can run this place as a bed and breakfast." Amy immediately ran back and forth between the rooms, spouting off ideas so fast, Jillian could barely keep up.

Amy pointed to the living room. "Gramps can move into a room right here when he recuperates. Then over here," she pointed to the other side, "you make your room. Look, there's plenty of space between for closets and a bathroom."

"That's a good idea," said Brad. "I think I could make it work."

Amy stopped and glanced at her watch. "Shoot. I've got to make deliveries. You two are going to have to finish up the details. I can't wait to hear all about it." In a flash, she was sprinting through the front door and calling out her good-byes as she crossed the yard.

Jillian's eyebrows knit together tightly as she tried to wrap her head around everything. Build new rooms. Rent the upstairs. Bring Gramps home from the rehabilitation center. *Seems like a pretty tall order.*

"You look a little worried," said Brad.

"That's an understatement. I never would have thought of this. Frankly, I'm wondering if I can pull it off."

"The way I see it, you're a mom, and Amy said you have lots of accounting experience, right?"

"True."

"So you're used to taking care of other people and juggling a million things at once. Sounds to me like you've got what it takes."

"Amy sure seems confident. I just need to think things through and weigh it out on paper. It's a really great idea, Brad, and I hope I'm up for it. I'm running out of options at this point."

After promising she wouldn't hold him to it, Jillian pushed Brad to give her a ballpark number. She wasn't surprised when he said he thought it would take about two hundred thousand dollars. It was tough to remain positive, especially with limited savings and no full-time employment on the horizon.

Her head was spinning with outcomes that all seemed to point at failure. She clearly didn't have enough money. Thanks to Chad, her days as comptroller at the firm were probably over. She would likely be blackballed and unable to find a position comparable to the one she worked her ass off to get at Prescott and Moore. She couldn't afford to spend the rest of her life processing taxes for a franchise operation in a long-forgotten strip mall. She saw herself watching through a dingy window as a costumed Statue of Liberty contorted himself, just for honks. Imagining her life in a rundown apartment with leaky windows and a greasy landlord made her shiver. Her reinvention wasn't going to be a pretty picture.

After brainstorming with Brad, Jillian drove back to Annapolis, picked up her daughter, and headed to the airport. Maegan was meeting ten other high school seniors who were going to study in Spain for the remainder of the year. Jillian wondered where Maegan got her sense of adventure. Ever since she was approached about early graduation and going to Spain, Maegan was on board. The kid had no fear. Jillian remembered being afraid of everything at her age. She didn't even want to leave high school. It was the same fear that held her back from many dreams over the years.

"Mom, I'm sorry about everything that's happening. I wish there was something I could do," Maegan said.

"There is. You have big plans. You're leaving for Spain, and you've worked really hard for it. You got a scholarship, saved your money, and set yourself up for success. When this plane takes off, all I want you to be thinking about is making your time in Spain the best ever. Don't spend one second worrying about me or Gramps. I've got a plan, and I think it's going to work. I just want you to be happy with your world, OK?"

"I will, Mom, promise."

Jillian embraced her daughter. She relaxed into it, something she didn't often allow herself the pleasure of experiencing. There were times when an extended hug could make her cry, and Jillian didn't want her daughter to know how mushy she really was. Maegan's hair—soft against Jillian's face—smelled of peaches and mint. Jillian breathed it in, felt her throat constrict, and choked back tears. Maegan's grip tightened, squeezing Jillian harder. They kissed good-bye, and Meagan ran to join her friends. Jillian watched her daughter's backpack disappear into the throng of travelers.

In the midst of bad judgement, emotional drama, and overwhelming confusion, Maegan was reaching for her dreams and making them happen. She hadn't been dragged down by the trash. Jillian slowly pulled away from the airport thinking, *When I grow up, I want to be just like her.*

Filled with apprehension, she drove to Prescott and Moore for her appointment with the company's founder. She prayed that the twelve years she and her husband, Chad, had worked for the large law firm would count for something. Chad had even made partner last year. But during the current year's audit, a stern-faced member of the auditing team had handed Jillian a file outlining $493,000 of expenses with documentation they found questionable. It was Jillian's job to find the answers, but at the time, she had no idea the assignment would turn her entire life upside down.

Seated now in Conference Room A, perspiration trickled behind her ear and left a skinny, wet trail to her collar. Jillian knew the report she turned in weeks ago would end her career. But there was no escaping the fact Chad had embezzled the funds, and she hadn't hesitated to lay out the evidence and turn it over to the auditing firm. She had known nothing about his crime, but it wouldn't matter.

The folder in front of her contained her letter of resignation. Being associated with Chad and his despicable choices made her feel ashamed and full of self-doubt. Despite a stomach that was voicing its displeasure by grumbling and cramping, she kept her back straight, shoulders squared, and head tall. She was ready, or at least pretended she was.

The door opened with a soft swish across the expensive carpeting. Mr. Moore greeted her with a solemn nod and took a seat.

"When we were originally notified there was a problem, we thought perhaps you were complicit. But when we received your final report, we were impressed with the level of detail you included and presented so honestly. It became clear that you were also a victim of Chad's decisions. I can't imagine how difficult it was for you to turn this in. You could have covered for him but chose not to. Instead, you did the right thing, and we believe your actions deserve consideration. I hope you will find the terms agreeable?"

He slid a document across the table toward Jillian. The firm had been generous. Six months of salary, her accrued vacation time, and a full year of health insurance for her and Maegan. Jillian's analytical brain ran the numbers through her internal calculator. *It was a start.*

"Mr. Moore, I'm thankful for your offer. I want to reiterate that I had nothing to do with this, and I'm sorry it happened. Under the circumstances, is there any possibility of acquiring a letter of recommendation to assist me in securing new employment?"

"I'll be frank, Jillian, it was discussed. . . ." His voice trailed off. The answer was obvious. Jillian stood and walked over to shake his hand. She quietly thanked him before taking her leave.

Jillian returned to her house in Annapolis for the night. After packing her belongings, she was exhausted and turned in early, but even in sleep, her mind was in overdrive. She tossed left, then right, face-down, then flipped to her back. The couch squeaked and groaned with every shift, and she woke, drenched in perspiration. Unrelenting thoughts flooded her brain, and she didn't have the power to fight them. When the rich chimes in the living room sang out two o'clock, she finally gave up, left the demons behind, and walked to the kitchen.

Jillian pulled out a pad and a pen. For a while, she simply sat and stared at them. It seemed the hardest thing in the world to face was a blank sheet of paper.

She was angry. Angry at Chad for taking it all away. Angry at her parents for being dead. Angry that Gramps had let his house go for so long. She was just plain angry, but mostly with herself. That anger forced her to try driving the plan down on paper. With one hand on a calculator and the other gripping a pencil, she scratched away the night.

Even though it needed repair, a house near the ocean in Rehoboth was worth a lot. She knew Gramps would agree to a home equity mortgage to cover the renovations, and she could make the payments with her money from the firm and some savings. Jillian's flicker of hope started to grow as she played with the numbers. There wouldn't be anything left at the end of each month, but with a lot of sacrifice, it could work. The ideas she cobbled together added up to almost two hundred thousand dollars.

It was a huge risk. Jillian sighed deeply. *It's not a matter of whether or not I can do it,* she thought, *I have to do it.* It was up to her to make sure Gramps didn't spend the rest of his life at the nursing home, and it was time for her to make a future for herself.

As the sun came up, she blinked at several pages filled with scribbles, clouds, directional arrows, and words. Her brain was exhausted, but the path she had forged to move ahead was formidable. Finally, the numbers were adding up. In the darkest moment during her lonely struggle, she realized she was more terrified of where she was than she was of failing on the way to something new. She had to move quickly to get to a better place, and any place would be better than the one she was in.

Jillian called Brad and asked, "How soon can you start?"

"We can be at your door Monday, bright and early."

Jillian arrived Sunday to clean up for the contractors. As darkness crept in, she noticed that the only working light downstairs was the one in the old range hood. She left it on and prayed the bulb would last. Grabbing a bottle of wine, she retreated to the couch for the night. She slid off her shoes and unzipped her skirt. Absentmindedly, her fingers scratched the itchy, red indentations around her belly left behind by the too-tight waistband. She curled up with her fuzzy fleece throw and drank from the bottle next to her.

A foul odor teased Jillian's nostrils. Investigating its source, she concluded that as hard as she worked to sanitize the house, the couch had absorbed the scent of rotten debris. She made a mental note to get it out of the house. Jillian tried not to think about the decay in her own life, but it was impossible. It was like something you'd read in a novel. Girl meets boy. Falls in love. Gets married. Makes a family. Boy goes psycho. Girl is ruined. The End. But this was no novel—this was her life.

With each board that creaked, every field mouse that scratched, and all the memories that whispered to her, Jillian felt worse. When the last swig of Malbec was drained from the bottle, she finally cried herself into a fitful sleep.

Brad and his crew blew through the front door at seven thirty in the morning. Jillian greeted them with bad breath and swollen eyes.

Brad took in her disheveled appearance and said, "Whoa, tough night, huh?"

Jillian grunted her answer. "No hot water."

"Well, we can fix that," he said with a smile, "but it'll take some time. I'm thinking it's going to take us about four months to complete the first phase of your project. You've got the kitchen rehab, the spa bathroom we talked about, and fixing up the rooms upstairs—plus your suite down here and a bit of exterior work. I'll handle the electric work myself and oversee my own crew and the plumber. My primary focus for now is your kitchen. Your down payment should cover it, which will give you time to get the rest of the financing in order."

"Sounds like you've got everything under control," said Jillian. "I'm going back to sleep for a bit."

"Oh no you don't. I think the best medicine for you today is to get your hands dirty with the crew," said Brad, tossing a pair of new leather work gloves at Jillian. "Put these on."

"Oh," she stammered, "I'm not ... I won't be ... I. . . ."

"Put them on. It's tradition."

Jillian put on the gloves, and he led her into the dining room. He sent a worker to the breaker box. When Brad heard the whistle from downstairs, he flicked the wall switch on and off twice. No lights came on.

Gesturing for Jillian to stand back, he raised the sledgehammer. Jillian tried to interrupt, but Brad wasn't listening. He swung the hammer hard at the wall, and a huge chunk of plaster fell onto the floor.

"Brad," Jillian interrupted again, "stop."

He nodded at her, smiled one of those "Don't worry, pretty lady" smiles, and ignored her warning. This time, his sledgehammer sunk in, and a shower of sparks exploded from the hole. Brad leaped back and dropped the sledge.

"Damn!" he yelled. "What the hell?"

Jillian smirked. "I tried to tell you. All the lightbulbs are burned out, so you might need to actually test the electric before you start."

"Nice," he said. "Real nice."

"You sure it's a good idea for you to be in charge of the electric? Maybe we should rethink that," teased Jillian.

Once the electricity was certifiably turned off in the dining room, he handed her the sledgehammer. "Your turn," he prompted. "Have some fun."

Jillian had never swung a sledgehammer before. Surprisingly, it was the kind of brutal action she needed. With each swing, she felt stronger. A few short minutes later, her shoulders were trembling from the effort and sweat was running down her face, but she was calmer than she had been in weeks. Handing it back to Brad, she asked him to make his first order of business the hot water.

"We're gutting the bathroom upstairs, and the second bathroom isn't functional, so you're going to have to find another place to shower while we're in the middle of all of this."

"Oh my God. I have to take a bath today. I smell like a mule."

"All right. I suppose we can wait until tomorrow to start the bathroom. I'll fire up the water heater for you. But starting tomorrow, you won't be able to shower here for at least a couple of weeks."

As soon as the hot water was ready, Jillian rushed upstairs with her bath basket, towel, and a fresh change of clothes. She closed and locked both doors leading into the bathroom. Gleefully, she stripped off her grimy clothes and sank into a tub full of steaming water.

Jillian sucked in the warm air, filling her lungs and then holding her breath. After a long pause, she let the air out in a whoosh, draining a huge chunk of anxiety from her mind. Letting tension go was always difficult for her. Even though the bathroom was private and the water felt glorious, she couldn't fully relax. She sunk underwater—head and all—like she had as a child. Water blocked most of the external noise, but she could clearly hear the pulse of her own blood. Focusing on the rhythm, she tried to relax.

A huge crash from the adjacent bedroom shocked her, and she scrambled upright in the tub, choking on water she had sucked in through her nose.

Bang, bang, bang. Someone was pounding on the bathroom door.

"What?" she said. "What do you want?"

"Hey," said Brad. "Sorry to interrupt your lady time, but we found something here I think you should see."

"Unless it's buried treasure, I'll look at it when I'm done."

"Well, actually, it looks like it might be somebody's buried treasure. Some pretty cool stuff, and it looks really old."

"Fine," she said with a sigh. "No rest for the wicked. Isn't that what they say? I'll be out in a few."

She finished rinsing the soap from her nooks and crannies, stepped out of the tub, dried off, and put on clean clothes. She wrapped a towel turban-style over her dripping hair before she stepped into the bedroom. The whole crew was gathered around Brad.

"What is it?" she asked. "Is it really treasure?"

He held out an army-green metal box with strange hinges.

"It's an ammo box from World War II," said one of the guys. "They sell them in surplus stores. Looks like a real nice one."

"Is there ammo in it?" asked Jillian.

"Nah, no ammo, but there *is* a bunch of stuff in here. Take a look," said Brad, handing the box to her. "Someone put this here an awful long time ago and never came back for it."

"Where did you find it?"

"I stepped on a plank in the back bedroom, and the other end of it popped up, so I pulled it up to look."

"How curious." Jillian opened the box.

The collected items obviously held great sentimental value for someone. They were carefully tucked into what looked like a woman's silk scarf. A black-and-white photograph of a young beauty and her handsome boyfriend was the first thing Jillian saw. The young lovers were on the beach; their faces turned to kiss as the photographer snapped the shot. Innocence, devotion, and true love, with Rehoboth Beach as the backdrop. The photo was simply inscribed, J.N. + H.M. Jillian noticed the young woman's hair was swept back with the same scarf that had blanketed these treasures for decades. Reaching in, she pulled out an old tube of lipstick and opened it, revealing the bright-red color. Glancing back at the picture she said, "I'll bet this is the same lipstick she's wearing."

"What else is there?" asked Brad.

Jillian found it funny that the guys were all crowding her, as intrigued by the contents as she was. "Let's go downstairs and take a closer look."

In the dining room, she carefully removed the scarf and

realized it was cut in half. She spread it out on the table, gently tracing its tattered edge. Laying the photograph on the scarf, Jillian reached back into the box to remove the contents so they could all get a good look.

She pulled out a pair of torn movie tickets, a tiny silver metal purse that clinked against the bottom of the metal box as Jillian lifted it, a silver locket with a wisp of hair inside, and a small glass vial filled with sand and sealed with cork. Jillian wondered if perhaps the items were gathered to remember a special moment on the beach. An antique harmonica in its original box was played so often, the initials inscribed on it—J.N.—were barely visible. The last thing she pulled out was a USO pin.

"No big haul for us to steal, so let's get back to work," joked Brad. "Pretty cool, though."

"Thanks for bringing it to me. I think I'm going to try to find out who left it there and see if I can reunite the box with its owner."

"Women. Always romantic at heart. You'll be hard-pressed to find the owner now. They're either dead or have one foot in the grave," said Brad.

"You're a real optimist. Good to know."

"Keepin' it real. Don't want you getting your hopes up for nothing."

Jillian gathered all the mementos and put them back in the ammo box. Placing the collection on a shelf in the hall closet, she closed the door. The box was left in darkness again.

Jillian's Journal

January 29th

I decided to keep a journal. There's so much going on right now, I struggle to keep it all straight in my head. Gramps had a huge setback. He had a major stroke this time and isn't able to do anything without assistance. I visit every day to check on him, but they said he would likely be staying for a few months. He has plenty of company. Barb has been spending lots of time with him, too. It's so disappointing—we were so close to having him home. I'm still staying at Amy and Greta's house. They've been the best friends ever. I couldn't get through this without them. Each week it seems like there's a new crisis. Someone's foot went through the upstairs bathroom floor and broke through the living room ceiling, an entire five-gallon pail of exterior paint was spilled over the porch roof, the upstairs toilet wasn't sealed properly, and light fixtures arrived on time but were twice as big as advertised.

I'm trying to stay calm and iron out one wrinkle at a time. It's not all bad news. My Thermador Grand Pro stove showed up and it's beautiful. Of course, that joy didn't last long. Some of my new furniture arrived the same day—in the wrong fabric. Better not ask, "What's next?" I'm too afraid of what the answer will be.

Maegan is my saving grace. I love talking to her over the internet every Sunday. When I tell her about the latest catastrophes here, she finds it pretty amusing. I'm so tickled to hear about her adventures. This week she told me about the Girona Flower Festival. She said the old town was covered in flowers, and it was the most beautiful thing she had ever seen. I'm not telling her about Gramps. No sense in worrying her.

There is still plenty to do here, but the end is in sight. I'm looking forward to a week or so alone so I can move my things back in and get settled before I start looking for guests. It's always good to have a plan.

YOU BREAK IT, YOU BUY IT!

Tucking a stray brown curl behind her ear, Jillian caught a glimpse of her left hand and cringed. It looked bare and unfamiliar without wedding rings. Although months had passed since she last wore them, she still wasn't used to it. She plunged her unadorned hands deep into the spring dirt just as the phone started yelling at her. *So much for getting the new plants in the ground during my free hour.*

Gardening was proving to be much more difficult than she imagined, and she had a whole new appreciation for it. Brad was due to arrive any minute to finish the upstairs bathroom, and she was excited to move back in as soon as he finished. There would be no leftover energy for plants. She tried to ignore the persistent ring, but eventually huffed in defeat and picked up the phone with muddy hands. She groaned as the black grit eased its way into the crevices of the phone case. *No time like the present.*

"Hello, you have reached The Sea Sprite Inn. This is Jillian. Can I help you?" *Well that sounded awkward*, she thought. *I'll have to work on it.*

The responding voice sounded like an overly caffeinated teenager—high pitched, with a hint of whine—like kids when you've told them another bedtime story is out of the question.

"Hi! My name's Carol. I heard you're getting ready to

open. I did a little research, and I'd like to make you an offer. Would you consider letting me stay there next weekend? I could be your first guest."

There was still so much to do. Furniture was arriving daily. At least it was showing up with the correct fabric this time. Jillian had hovered over the delivery crews like a helicopter parent, trying to protect the newly finished floors. Baseboards and trim were yet to be painted. The punch list was dwindling, but the Sea Sprite wouldn't be ready for at least two weeks.

"I'm sorry, Carol. I'd love to, but I really can't."

"Actually, I'm not just any visitor," countered Carol. "It's a great time to visit the beach: stores are having pre-season sales, restaurants aren't full, and the beach isn't crowded. I'm a bargain shopper who's willing to negotiate. If you give me a little discount, I'll be your first guest—even with work going on—sort of like a test guest. I won't ask you to cook for me as long as I can have kitchen privileges. What do you say? Deal?"

"Well, I ..." stammered Jillian. "I really don't think. . . ."

"Pleeeaaasseee?"

Her voice was oozing with expectancy, and Jillian was too tired to argue. *I'm always too accommodating,* she thought. *On the other hand, this would be a great dry run.*

"OK, Carol. Tell you what. I'll give you a twenty percent discount as long as I don't have to cook."

"Deal! You won't regret it. I promise."

Jillian's agitation was expelled with a deep breath, and she tried out part two of her script: "Is there anything I can do to help make your stay special?" *That sounded pretty good.*

Carol's voice brightened. "I do have something in mind.

I was wondering if you know anyone who could take me out to catch my own fish. I love seafood, and I want to catch my own. Fishing charters are pretty pricey, so I thought maybe—just maybe—you would know someone who would be willing to give me a bargain."

Jillian thought about the request. The first person who came to mind was Rob, a friend from high school she had run into recently at an auction where she purchased an antique jewelry display case. The case was too big for Jillian's trunk, and he was kind enough to offer to move it for her. He owned a small charter fishing boat and, thankfully, a big truck. She was certain he would enjoy showing Carol the tricks of his trade. Jillian selfishly thought maybe he could even throw in some fish for her—as a referral bonus. "I'll make a couple of calls to see what I can do."

As she hung up the phone, Jillian reflected on the past four months. Brad's suggestion to turn the house into a bed and breakfast had come at the right time. She was in the midst of divorcing Chad and seeking to reinvent herself. After a home equity loan, a few mishaps, and an enormous amount of work, the place was livable again.

I can't believe it, Jillian thought. *The first guest is booked.*

Carol arrived on Saturday, smelling like a walking advertisement for Bath and Body Works. Her lips were painted with fuchsia sparkles that glinted with each smile. She spent the first forty-five minutes of her arrival showing Jillian all the bargains she had picked up at the outlets on the way down.

"Would you look at this?" She teased a huge silk scarf out of the bag first. "This gorgeous little piece of silk was only five dollars! You can't even touch a new one for under thirty bucks these days." She swirled it dramatically around her closely cropped, platinum-blonde hair before putting it on the table.

"And this purse?" Carol accentuated her bargain by using hand model gestures. "It's a Kate Spade. Retails for three hundred dollars. I paid thirty-two. Thirty-two!" She casually tossed it on top of the scarf.

"Hmm, you're quite a shopper," said Jillian.

"I know," said Carol. She fished a beach hat out of her bag, held it next to her neon-green Skechers to show the match, and threw it on top of the stack with a flourish. "Three dollars."

As the stack grew, Jillian's fidgeting increased. Finally, with the addition of six new discount bras, the entire pile toppled over, taking with it an expensive-looking glass shell lamp. Carol caught the lamp right before it hit the floor and simultaneously took note of Jillian's last thread of patience. "I'm sorry. I get so excited talking about my bargains. Sometimes I can't stop myself. It's such an adrenaline rush for me. But you must have a million things to do, so I'll go get my things settled and we can chat later."

Carol ran to her car and started carrying in reusable bags overflowing with produce. She hip-checked the rear door of the car, but it left her off-balance. Losing her grip on two bags, they dropped and spilled their contents onto the driveway. "Stopped by the farmers market and picked up some fresh veggies," she cheerily called out. "The prices were phenomenal!"

Jillian laughed. "Well, let's see if we can't get you hooked up with some fish to go with them."

The next day, Carol scoured local stores and returned to the Sea Sprite with her arms overloaded with more bargains.

"You sure love a good hunt, don't you," said Jillian. "You should try the Treasure Chest Thrift Shop. It's run by Beebe Hospital. I'll bet you would have a great time there."

"I'll definitely write that one down. You've got me pegged. I guess that's the reason I started my little antique business. Sifting through gently used trinkets and castaway belongings has always felt like a treasure hunt to me. But my favorite part is the people you meet."

"Since you like treasures so much, I should tell you about mine."

"Ohhh ... sounds interesting!" Carol set her recent haul on the stairs.

Jillian pulled out her treasure box. "My contractor found this box hidden under the floorboards upstairs. One of his workers said it was an old ammo box from World War II. I'm trying to figure out who it belongs to."

Carol touched the contents gingerly. "I'd say he's probably right. Looks like most of these things date back to the '30s or '40s. I've seen lots of these little USO pins. They were popular during the war. Do you have any leads yet?"

"No. I haven't had a lot of time to research it. I'm going to keep them in a jewelry display case I bought at the auction. Rob—the same guy who's taking you fishing—is delivering it for me tonight. If you're here, I'll introduce you," said Jillian.

"Sounds like great timing. I'd like to get to know him a little before we spend a whole day fishing," said Carol.

"He's laid back. His ex-wife wanted a fast-paced life, and they made a lot of quick moves that didn't work out. Rob decided that type of life wasn't for him."

"Sounds like me. I made a few quick moves that didn't work out—like marrying someone after a few months of dating. Not too bright," said Carol.

"Sounds like you've learned from it and are on a different path now, so that's a good thing," said Jillian.

❦

As Carol walked into the Treasure Chest Thrift Shop carrying several brightly patterned, well-worn, reusable shopping bags on her arms, one of the women behind the counter came out to greet her.

"Hi, my name is Marci. How can I help you?" Her smile was huge, and despite being middle-aged, she was bubbling over with the enthusiasm of a teenager.

"I'm going on a boat, but I have no idea what to wear."

"Ah. Cruise wear." Marci steered Carol through the store, assembling an outfit consisting of a pair of white clamdiggers, a turquoise linen shirt sporting a bold pattern in bright-orange and pink embroidery, a wide-brimmed straw sunhat, a jacket, and a pair of orange flip-flops.

"Oh, Marci, I love this. You've got a great eye."

Carol excitedly hugged the pieces to her chest and twirled, letting the clothes fly. She made it almost all the way around before a shirtsleeve caught the display rack and pulled her off-balance. Her bottom bumped the shelves. Both ladies shrieked as the entire display crashed to the floor with Carol's backside perched right on top of the "You Break It, You Buy It!" sign.

"Oh no," moaned Carol. "I'm sorry. What an awful mess."

Marci's eyes opened widely, and her perkiness dimmed

momentarily before she regained her sparkle. She darted to Carol's side and offered her a hand up.

"I think we should stick to bargain hunting and leave out the fancy footwork for now," she teased. "I thought for sure you were going to end up at the hospital, which is where I usually volunteer.

"I'm so sorry."

"I'm just glad you're not hurt."

Carol helped Marci clean up the mess. Standing at the register, she waited for the total of the day's expenses to reveal themselves:

hat, $4.00
clamdiggers, $4.50
shirt, $4.50
flip-flops, $3.00
jacket, $4.00

Carol calculated silently along with the cash register. *Wow,* she thought, *twenty bucks for a complete outfit is a great day.* Then she realized the register hadn't stopped tallying at the end of her pile. She watched, excitement bleeding out of her one item at a times as the damaged goods were added to her bill. When the total was revealed, Carol owed twenty dollars for her new outfit and an additional $135.50 for the damage caused by her big hips.

Carol graciously thanked Marci for all her help and patience, paid for her items (plus the twirling tax), and walked out with her bags filled with intentional—and unintentional—purchases. Although the day hadn't turned out the way she expected, she figured it was worth it. After all, how could she possibly feel bad when her "donation" would benefit the hospital?

Back at the Sea Sprite, she squeezed through the door, backside first, with her overflowing bargain bags, bumping into something solid behind her.

"Hey!" said a startled male voice.

"Oops, sorry," said Carol with an embarrassed smile.

"Not a graceful entrance, but your timing is impeccable," added Jillian. "Carol, this is Rob."

Rob, slightly chubby for a boat captain, extended a tanned, well-worn hand. Deep crevices divided his cheeks, and bushy, brown eyebrows shielded narrow eyes. His dark hair was parted deeply on the side, and he reminded Carol of a celebrity—she couldn't remember which one.

"Nice to meet you," Carol said. "Wait 'till you hear what happened to me." She traipsed into the gathering room and set her bags down on the couch with an exasperated sigh.

"Rob was nice enough to deliver my latest purchase and set it up for me," said Jillian.

"Oh, right," Carol said. "Now I remember—the jewelry case."

"Since I'm here, we should set a time for your fishing trip," said Rob.

"Great idea," said Carol, "but first, I have to tell you guys what happened today. You won't believe it."

As she vented, Carol seemed to relax a little. She loved an audience. Both Rob and Jillian seemed captivated by her story. When she described herself landing on top of the entire heap of broken display pieces and various trinkets, Rob let loose with a deep belly laugh and Jillian joined in. "There I was, on the floor, with a sign that read 'You Break It, You Buy It!' sticking out from under my behind." Carol couldn't help but laugh along with them as she recalled what a sight she must have been.

When Carol finished, Rob asked, "What do you say we head out early tomorrow morning to get your fishing trip in?" Jillian politely excused herself and left the two of them alone to discuss the details.

"What's your definition of early?" Carol asked. "I need my beauty sleep."

"That's fair. So I'm guessing you're a sleepy lady at dawn," he joked. "I usually start at five, but how about I pick you up at seven? It's a little ride to the Indian River Marina, where my girl is docked, and I can pick you up on the way."

Carol was caught off guard. "I won't pay full price for sharing this trip with your *girl*. I'm looking for private fishing lessons and a guarantee I'll come home with enough fish for a nice meal or two."

"No guarantees in fishing, but you'll be the only customer," he said, and walked away.

She followed, trying to bring him back into the conversation.

"OK, I suppose seven is fine. I should be up by then, and I'll be ready to go. Do you have any tips for me? Any suggestions? Any pointers or advice?"

"Nope. Don't suppose I do," he answered brusquely. "Just be ready to go, and we'll make a morning of it."

He hadn't even stopped. Instead, he kept walking toward the door. Carol strode through the foyer to make sure her comments weren't being ignored. As she drew closer, she kept her eyes on him, trying to figure out why he had suddenly lost interest. She was close enough now to reach out and touch his arm, which she did. But when her fingers detected the heavily muscled arm under his shirt and he turned to look at her, she forgot what she had planned to say.

"I see," she managed. "Tomorrow it is. Bright and early." He nodded his head in agreement, and she detected a slight smile before he continued to the door. Carol spun around quickly, promptly stubbing her big toe on Jillian's new display case. "Ouch!" she yelped. "What the hell? I suppose it was your idea to put this here?" She plopped down next to the offending furniture to tend to her toe.

Rob came over, knelt down, and gently took her foot in his hand. He bent each of her toes back and forth and carefully turned her ankle in a circular motion. "No need to get all worked up over it; nothing is broken," he said, as if rendering a verdict.

"Gee, thanks."

"Looks like you create problems wherever you go. You might want to stop twirling in small areas."

"Real funny. It's just been an unusual day." Although, when she thought about it, she did see an embarrassing pattern.

What is that sound? Oh God, is it six already? Carol battled through her groggy sleep coma, grabbed the phone, and turned off the annoying alarm. Today was a new day. She had the chance to make it extra productive and special. Today she would catch her own fish.

Carol emerged from the bathroom decked out in her new Treasure Chest finds and stumbled sleepily down the stairs. She heard the back door open and Jillian's soft voice welcoming Captain Rob. She smelled fresh coffee and rolls. She made her way to the kitchen and smiled gratefully at Jillian through hazy lids. "You are an angel. You have no idea how much I need this coffee." She saw Rob's eyes glide over her turquoise top, past the white pants, and down to the orange flip-flops. He slowly shook his head.

"What?"

"What is that you're wearing?"

"Oh, this?" Carol said proudly. "It's my fishing excursion ensemble. Do you like it?"

"Well, it's colorful, I'll say that. But for catching fish, you want to wear dark, dull colors. The bright ones tend to scare the fish away. And as for flip-flops—they aren't safe on a boat."

"Well, I think the fish will be attracted to my bright colors, and flip-flops are comfy for me."

"Suit your fancy, then. Just don't say I didn't warn ya."

Carol rolled her eyes at him and smiled brightly at Jillian while announcing, "Fish for dinner. My treat." She swept out the door and Rob followed, giving her a lift into the huge truck. She teased, "You need a ladder for this thing!" Chuckling, he closed her door before climbing in behind the wheel.

"So I've got a Grady-White Express 330," he said as he guided the truck smoothly toward Route 1. "Got a forty-five-gallon live-well built into the starboard side. On the other side, she's got a rigging station with cutting board, tackle center, and sink. She's a dream for real fishermen."

Carol mumbled a polite, "hmmm."

Rob droned on, "The builders didn't stop there. Oh, no. They built a large cabin underneath with A/C. The galley works for fixing anything from quick bites to full meals. There are two double berths. The head even has a sink, shower, and storage."

"Sorry, what? I must have drifted off there for a second."

"Nice. Wait till you see her; you'll love her."

"Her?"

"Yes, my boat—the 'girl' you thought I was bringing along. She's a real beauty."

As Rob turned off onto Inlet Road, Carol opened her purse and took out her phone to take some pictures of the marina. Colorful flags flew on a few of the masts; some had red lanterns strung up on the decks, and others were spectacular just as they were.

Carol put the phone in her lap and turned to Rob. "Does your boat have a name?"

"Yup, she sure does. *Shark Bait.*"

"Wait, you named your boat *Shark Bait*? Does that refer to your female guests or to what happens to them when they fish with you?"

Rob grinned. "Definitely not the former. We'll have to see about the latter after we finish today."

When the truck was parked, Carol—excited to begin her adventure—opened her door and swung her legs to the side. Without a thought about the height of the massive truck, she leaped from her seat. That's when she saw her sparkly phone launch from her lap and land with a crunch in the gravel at Rob's feet. He had rushed around the truck to help her, but he arrived too late to rescue the phone. He picked it up to examine the damage.

"I hope you're due for an upgrade."

"Dang it. I totally forgot it was in my lap," she said as she took in the spider-web fractures covering the screen. "Now how am I going to get pictures of my trip?"

"No worries; we can use mine. But don't forget: you break it, you buy it."

Carol—her enthusiasm dampened slightly—boarded *Shark Bait*, taking Rob's hand to steady herself. As soon as her first foot landed on the deck, Rob said, "Remember: you break it, you buy it."

She rolled her eyes at him. "Really? Is it necessary to keep reminding me? Will you stop saying it if I agree to buy anything I break?"

Rob shrugged with a laugh and said, "From what I've witnessed, I should probably make signs and post one everywhere you walk."

"Oh boy, a comedian disguised as a fishing captain. What more could I ask for?"

"So this is the deck. We'll be fishing from here." He walked to the stairs and led Carol under the deck to the berths.

"Wow, I had no idea it would be this big. And it's clean. I'm impressed." She saw Rob blush. "I do have one question. Where's the bathroom?"

Rob slid a pocket door to the side and revealed a tiny room with a shower and toilet in it. "This is the head, err, bathroom."

Carol gave Rob a lingering appraisal, running her eyes over his large frame, and said, "You? Fit in there?"

"Now who's the comedian," said Rob. He climbed the stairs and took his place behind the controls.

"Can I borrow your phone to take a few pictures of the boat?"

Rob scrunched up his face as though he were really debating the answer and feared for the safety of his phone.

"Here." He handed the phone to her. "But you know the deal."

Carol stuck her tongue out at him and then smiled.

"We're going to head over to the Old Grounds today." Rob started the engine. "Reef sites 10 and 11 have a lot of flounder waiting on us. We'll back-drift over them. I brought several different types of bait, but let's start with minnows. He reached over and opened the top of a bucket to show her.

"Live fish?"

"Uh, yeah."

"Ewww."

Rob laughed. "I've also got an artificial bait called Gulp. I'm not real sure how it works, I only know it does."

"I'll take that," said Carol.

When they reached the fishing spot, Rob stopped the engine and called Carol over to the back of the boat.

"Flounder are a different kind of fish," he said as he prepared her rod. "They lie on the bottom and try to ambush their prey. You have to be a little patient—not your strength, based on what I've seen. Your best bet is to bump the bait right over their heads, annoying them—now there's something you do well—and then they'll take the bait."

"Got it."

"The most important pointer is, don't jerk your line trying to set the hook right away like you normally do with fish. If you wait until they swallow the bait and then set your line, you'll have a much better chance of having flounder for dinner. Got it?"

"Got it."

"And don't let them get too close to the boat without setting the hook 'cause if they see what you're wearing, they'll be gone in a jiffy."

"Right. So if we don't catch anything, you're going to blame it all on my outfit. I can hear it now."

"The first few times, we'll try it together." Rob stepped closer to Carol and handed her the rod. "Have you ever fished before?"

"I used to fish when I was young, but I haven't done it in years."

"Well, the good news is, it's like riding a bike. You never really forget how to do it once you've learned. I'll let you cast the first one on your own, and then I'll help you learn the feel of the set with me."

Carol gingerly took the rod and cast her first line. It landed about two feet from the boat.

"Must be those flip-flops holding you back."

"I'll tell you where you can put my flip-flops," said Carol as she cautiously readied herself for the second cast.

Holding the rod with her right hand, she tugged on the line until she had some hanging out. She pressed it down with the crook of her index finger and opened the bail. She could feel his eyes, and a wave of pride washed over her. She pointed the rod directly at her target and lifted it to vertical. Letting it flex back behind her, she cast the rod forward in a beautiful arc, let go of the line, and watched the bait land right where she had aimed.

"That's it." Rob stepped in behind her and guided his arms around her. He placed his hands over hers and made the bait jump across the bottom of the water with little flicks of his wrists. Carol tried to maintain focus on the feel of the rod in her hands. She felt the resistance the second it happened. He held her hands steady and whispered, "Yep, that's it. He's checking it out. Be patient. Wait ... wait ... take your time."

Carol held her breath, trying to feel the change in the line and picturing the flounder nibbling on the bait. She waited.

Rob counted, "OK, we're gonna set the hook in five, four, three, two. . . ." Carol couldn't wait. With a solid yank, she lifted the rod quickly and felt the pull of the fish on the line.

"I think you got him," cheered Rob. "Could've been a little more patient, but you got him. Now reel him in slowly." He grabbed the net, scooped up her catch, and brought it onto the boat.

"Will you look at that? Damn, girl, he looks like a doormat. You got him on your second cast. That's gotta be unheard of. Let's measure this bad boy."

Rob deftly removed the bait and hook from Carol's flounder and placed the fish on the measuring stick. Carol flushed with excitement.

"He's 24 ½ inches. That has to be five pounds of fish right there. Grab my phone and let's get some pictures."

Carol bent down and reached to hand Rob his phone. When their hands met, the flounder took a huge leap, and its tail smacked Carol in the face. She stumbled and stepped on the discarded bait pulled from her fish's mouth. As soon as her foot hit the slimy mess, she knew what was coming next. Carol's flip-flops betrayed her, and her feet went straight up in the air. The rest of her flipped under, crashing to the deck.

Briefly, Carol managed to stay focused and yell, "Catch!"

to Rob, before tossing him his cell phone in what would later be described as a top ten "Play of the Day" move. The phone landed solidly in Rob's free hand. At the same time, Carol's arm hit the cooler, and her head cracked loudly against the deck.

She looked up at Rob anxiously as he gingerly touched her arm. Worry seemed to pour from every inch of him. "We're gonna get you to Beebe, and they'll fix you up good as new, OK? Just hang with me, and I'll get you there." He started the engine, turned the boat around, and headed back to the dock at top speed.

After a painfully bumpy ride in the fast-moving truck, Carol saw the sign for Beebe Hospital and Rob drove them to the emergency entrance. He jumped from the truck and grabbed a wheelchair.

Several hours and many painkillers later, Carol woke in a hospital bed with her head bandaged and a sling on her arm. She was surprised to see Marci—the volunteer from the hospital's thrift shop—dozing in the chair next to her. When Carol cleared her throat, Marci instantly sat up, on alert.

"Hey, lady, how are you feeling?" Marci asked. "I saw you come in, so I thought I'd pop by and say hello."

"Umm, I've felt better," mumbled Carol. "I guess I've done it again, and I wasn't even twirling."

"It looks like a possible concussion and a sprained wrist this time. Doctor said she'll have you out of here soon. She wanted to keep a close eye on you for a bit since you took quite a fish whipping."

"Boy, did I ever." Carol rallied. "Where's Rob? Did I ruin everything?"

"You didn't ruin a thing. In fact, he's on his way back

to see you. He stayed here until the doctor was sure you were all right, and then he zoomed out of here on some important mission." Marci was interrupted by a knock.

They looked up to see Rob smiling at the door. Marci leaned over and whispered, "Looks like my cue to leave." She smiled and gave a quick wave, closing the door as she left.

After an "all clear" from the hospital, Rob delivered Carol to the Sea Sprite, where Jillian had prepared a surprise. The table was set, and a steaming platter of flounder with lemon butter sauce and fresh grilled zucchini waited for them.

"Oh, no. I promised you wouldn't have to cook."

"Don't be silly. It's the least I can do when someone brings home a catch like this. I hope you're feeling better." Jillian seated them, filled their glasses, and quietly left the kitchen.

Out of habit, Carol reached for the serving fork.

"Ow!"

"Not so fast there. Let me serve it." Rob filled the waiting plates and added, "Thanks for saving my phone. It was quite a heroic effort for a piece of overrated electronics."

"You're welcome. Sorry I didn't listen to you about the flip-flops."

"No need to apologize. A better captain wouldn't have let you on his boat in flip-flops, knowing how dangerous they are."

"Thanks," said Carol.

"I'm not sure if the catch of the day was my phone or this delicious fish. But we do need to square up the bill."

"The bill?"

"Remember? You break it, you buy it. You landed on my cooler and it's busted."

She grinned. "Well, I have expert witnesses willing to testify that it was *you* who busted *me* by leaving slimy bait on the deck. Plus, if it weren't for my mad fishing skills, we wouldn't be having this great meal. The way I look at it, you owe me."

"I have to admit, this was one of the biggest flounder caught on my boat yet."

"Uh-huh. Usually, the best ones get away, but not this time."

"That's right. You're still here." Rob leaned a little closer and said, "I think we should try it again, just to see if you're as good as you think you are." They grinned at each other.

"I'd love that, but I promise from now on, I'll be patient— and no flip-flops."

"Well, well, well," Rob said. "Now I definitely know what the catch of the day was."

Carol grinned. *I'm going to be patient, all right,* she thought. *I've got a feeling this one might be worth reeling in slowly.*

Jillian's Journal

May 16th

I can't believe the Sea Sprite is open! Even though I expected Carol to be a distraction, she actually turned out to be a joy. I'm glad I decided to take the reservation—it was good to make sure the inn is ready to open, and she surprised me by teaching me a thing or two.

My takeaways:

One – I need to look more closely at what I acquire. Now I realize I can get exactly what I want, as long as I take my time.

Two – I never would have thought of going on a fishing trip for myself. Carol truly embraced it and even came back with a fish. Now I'm thinking about things I may want to do that I've never considered before because I classified them as activities for men, younger people, or even older people. Things I have never considered doing may be a chance for growth. Surfing? Skydiving? Horseback riding? The possibilities are endless.

I'm so happy with the antique jewelry display case I found at the auction. It will be a handy place for drinks and snacks, and I can't wait to put the trinkets from the ammo box in it. I'm so relieved Carol didn't tip it over.

This morning, Brad and his crew hung The Sea Sprite Inn sign, making it official. I've got my fingers crossed. I sure hope that little sprite will bring me some luck.

ON THE STAND

Fruit flies, of all things. The tiny black pests sped through the air like well-trained pilots anxious to dive-bomb into the fresh strawberries Jillian had carefully picked from the garden. The warm May breeze carried the heavy scent of their ripe sweetness. Jillian plopped down in the glossy black side chair and sank deeply into its marshmallow cushion. Her hand slowly fanned back and forth, protecting the berries on the teal side table from the drunken flies.

The hideaway garden was identified by an intentionally aged whitewashed sign that read, "The Gathering Glen." Its lavender lettering looked quaint and whimsical against the periwinkle paint coating the Sea Sprite's trim. Jillian's favorite spot in the glen was partly shaded by a large, ornamental cherry tree. A bird gleefully flip-flopped in the bath under the branches, sending glittery water diamonds into orbit with its contorted gyrations.

Jillian's gaze flowed over the stepping-stone path flanked with ivy and newly planted annuals. Yard hooks bent under the weight of hanging flower baskets filled with purple petunias and lobelia. Barb had grumbled about the plants when Jillian brought them home.

"Honey," she said. "I'm sure they looked pretty at the store, but they're not going to survive a month where you've put them."

Jillian had promised from now on, she would consult with Barb's green thumb before doing any more amateur gardening. Casually allowing her mind to wander, she popped a juicy strawberry into her mouth and smiled when it burst, rewarding her with seasonal juice. *At least I got the strawberries right.* The phone rang, startling her from her reverie.

"Hi, you called The Sea Sprite Inn. Are you ready for a vacation?" *That seemed a little off,* thought Jillian. *I need to come up with something better.*

"Boy, are we ever," the caller said, playing along. "I'm wondering if you have availability for three of us in two rooms for next week."

Jillian paused and quickly calculated whether or not Brad would have the second bedroom finished by then. She really needed to fill another week. Taking a huge leap of faith, Jillian answered, "Yes, we can give you two rooms next week."

"Great. We finally get a break. My daughter's a competitive swimmer, and we could use a vacation from all these swim meets. My name's Darla Anderson. It'll be my husband, myself, and our daughter, Maddie."

After processing the deposit, Jillian asked, "Is there anything I can help with to make your stay special?"

"Not that I can think of at this moment. I'm assuming there are lots of things a teenager can keep herself busy with and not get into too much trouble?"

Jillian laughed. "I suppose it depends on the teenager you're talking about. But in general, there are plenty of fun things for kids here, especially around the boardwalk, which is only a couple of blocks away."

"Sounds great. Maybe my husband and I will grab a little time to do our own exploring."

"I'm sure you can make that happen. I look forward to meeting you next week."

New to her innkeeper role, Jillian realized she had forgotten to ask how they found out about theSea Sprite, along with another five or six questions she should have asked. *There's a learning curve and I'm definitely on it.* Jillian finished the reservation and found herself happy at the prospect of having a teenage girl around the inn—even if it was someone else's daughter.

SLAM. The back door of the Sea Sprite shook in its frame. Maddie's arms pumped air with each swing, and her feet stomped impressions into the soft grass. "Humph," she huffed, glaring back toward the door. She simultaneously regretted slamming the door and wished she had done it hard enough to shatter the glass. *Why didn't they understand? Would they ever stop pushing?*

She had overheard her parents talking with the inn's owner about her lack of a social life. The last line sent her over the edge. "She's not your average teenager." Why couldn't they get that her life would be hell when Coach G got her back in the pool?

When her parents suggested the vacation, Maddie wasn't sure she could really take time away from her swimming regimen. She had worked too hard, for too many years, to focus on anything but her goal of beating the University of Virginia women's record in the two hundred meter freestyle. It was so weird. Sometimes her parents seemed like they were all into her swimming. Like how her mom always yelled louder than anyone from the sidelines: "Go, Maddie, it's all you. Go!" God, it was so embarrassing.

But now, Maddie decided that coming along was a big mistake. It felt like her parents were working really hard to soften her and force her to have fun. They disguised their efforts by saying that meeting new people would make her "well-rounded" and "balanced." Did that mean without a boyfriend she was unbalanced?

As Maddie sat, she saw the owner crossing the lawn with a glass of lemonade. Her breathing slowed, and her shoulders dropped their defensive position.

"You must be Maddie. I'm Jillian," the woman said, setting the glass down slowly on the table.

"Nice to meet you." Maddie noticed Jillian seemed focused on a pair of hummingbirds that were zipping in and out of the bright red and orange flowers next to the table.

"You've got to ask yourself how they know which flowers to choose. Maybe my friend was right after all. These hummingbirds always seem to show up at just the right time." Cocking her head at an angle with a puzzled look, Jillian went back inside the house.

Maddie watched for several moments, waiting for the hummingbirds to come back. When they didn't return, she rose in one fluid motion and walked back to the porch door. She paid a retroactive apology to it by opening it, stepping inside, and gently pulling it closed with reverence.

Hearing voices in the reception area, Maddie peeked around the corner in time to watch her parents exiting the inn's front door. She paused until the coast was clear and spotted stacks of pastries, cheeses, cookies, and fruit—and a comfy chair she could plop into. She gently coughed to announce her presence.

"Hello again," said Jillian, lifting her gaze over the top of the computer to connect with Maddie's big hazel eyes.

"Hi, Jillian. I'm ... uh ... sorry about slamming your door before. It's just that, well, my parents really ticked me off."

"OK," Jillian began slowly, "apology accepted. Try to remember that this is a business, and I have other people staying here. They expect peace and relaxation, not mercurial teenagers who slam doors during tantrums."

Maddie slunk down into the overstuffed white cushions of the chair nearest the desk. "You're right. I'm sorry."

"Look, you don't know me very well, but I have a daughter, too. Maegan's seventeen, about the same age you are. Your parents ... oh, by the way, your parents left for the outlets. They said to tell you you're on your own today."

"Good." Maddie exhaled with relief.

"They'll be back around dinnertime. Anyway, back to parents. As a parent, I try to do my best. It's my job to point out times when I think Maegan's doing something that's not in her best interest. I'm not always right, but I always have the best intentions."

"I've tried to do the things they ask me to do. It's a waste of time. They wanted me to go out with some guys, so I tried going out. You wanna know what happened? My first date tried to arm-wrestle me, and he never called again. The second guy? He said he loved to work out, so we went to the gym together. As soon as I took off my jacket and he saw my shoulders, he said he wasn't feeling good. We didn't even make it through the first set."

"So two dates and you're finished with the dating scene?"

"I didn't say I was finished. I'm sick of being pushed into it. I've been swimming and winning competitions my whole life. It feels great. I know all the swimmers, the coaches, and the parents. I don't need new people. It's stupid."

"So you're happy with the way things are?"

"Mostly. I mean, sometimes I wish I was just a regular girl. It's just dumb. Who wants to hang out with a female jock who trains all the time because she wants to beat a school record?"

Jillian paused a moment before responding. "Maddie, how did you learn to swim so well?"

"Coaches, mostly."

"So those coaches tell you what to do to improve and you do it, right?"

"Yep."

"You're getting close to the record, right?"

"Right. I only need to shave off a few more seconds."

"I'm sure it's taken a load of hard work and lots of stress. But what about fun?"

"There will be time for fun after I win. Right now, I need to stay focused on my goal."

"Do you know much about hummingbirds? I don't. But a friend of mine told me that if a hummingbird shows up, it's to remind you to cherish the simple pleasures in life and that you need to take time to enjoy yourself. Believe whatever you want, but you saw the hummingbirds outside. Maybe those birds are here to remind you that you need a little fun. Your parents are trying to help you build a life, and they have a lot of experience."

"OK, well, thanks. I'll think about it. I've gotta get my workout in. I just wanted to say sorry for the door slamming thing." *Hummingbirds,* thought Maddie. *I think she's lost it.*

"Enjoy your workout," Jillian called to the back of her head. Maddie was already bounding up the steps to her room.

Maddie hurried to make up for lost time. The Lycra shorts slid up her long legs, easily stretching over the muscular curves it had taken so many tears to develop. Pulling the workout tank over her head, Maddie inhaled an unpleasant whiff of yesterday's workout. *Darn, I thought this made it to the hamper yesterday.* Fumbling around in her suitcase, she felt the slick polyester of another tank and exchanged rank for refreshed. She laced her cross trainers tightly and rushed out of the room. *Some vacation this is.* She went out the back door with her yoga mat and navigated to the most level spot she could find.

In a seated position, Maddie went through the stretching routine on autopilot. First, her neck, shoulders, and arms. The hips and legs followed. Her first reach for the toes, she heard her back pop. With each outward breath, the stretches grew deeper. Muscles elongated and gave up their regimented hold. Thirty minutes exactly. Maddie smiled and stood at the ready.

Her dryland routine consisted of core work, squat jumps, lateral jumps, tuck jumps, alternate leg bounding, and burpees. She kept a notebook and recorded each activity. The cover was marked in bold, red letters, "Land Torture." Completing anything that was done out of the water caused Maddie pain, but the exercises were mandatory and a necessary evil to keep her in shape for the trials, so she was driven to complete them. At the same point during her workouts, she asked herself, who the hell invented burpees, and how can I find them and kill them?

Finished with land torture, all that remained was her morning run. Maddie headed under the flowered arch and onto the driveway. As she walked briskly on the uneven gravel, rocks poked into the thin sole of her shoes, reminding her that caution was necessary. Ever since Maddie was little, her runs began the same. In her head, she could hear the whistle blow. Then, the music would play in her mind, and her feet would start stamping at the fastest speed she could muster. After calling out "Yabba dabba doooo!" she would begin her run in earnest. Settling in during her first strides, she would sing to herself. "Flintstones, meet the Flintstones, they're the modern Stone Age family. . . ." She remembered Saturday mornings with her parents. Mom would make French toast, and they would all cuddle on the couch watching *The Flintstones*. Later in the day—when she ran with her dad—he would always start by mimicking Fred Flintstone's work whistle, and then they would start running while singing the cartoon's theme song.

She had four miles today and plenty of thoughts to keep herself company. Heading down Olive Avenue, she spotted another runner coming toward her. Even from a distance, she could tell he was in great shape. His red shorts looked familiar. Maybe he was a lifeguard. That would make sense since he was so fit. In fact, he would have presented the perfect picture if his running stance hadn't looked so weird. He held his arms up like a chicken with his wrists limply dangling at the ends. It almost made Maddie laugh. As they passed each other, he waved and grinned widely, showing a set of excellent teeth, which Maddie was picky about. Teeth can tell you all you need to know about people's hygiene. Her mom taught her that. She waved back and smiled. She kept running, thinking about how cute he was—with the exception of the chicken wings, of course, which were pretty tough to ignore.

Pounding back through the flowered arch at the Sea Sprite, Maddie felt much better. Endorphins carried her, and she was thankful for their help. The rest of the day was entirely open, and after a quick shower, she was going to the beach. It was bound to be jam-packed, and the people-watching would be excellent. She grabbed her UVA duffle bag and stuffed a towel, water bottle, hair ties, and her Kindle inside.

She met Jillian in the hallway. "Hi, I'm heading out to the beach for a little while. I'll be back around four. Is that OK?" It felt strange not to have to report her comings and goings to anyone. Maddie wasn't sure why she had appointed Jillian as a substitute parent, but she had.

Jillian smiled. "Good for you. Have fun."

⌐┬

He was there, on the stand. Chicken-wing guy was a lifeguard after all. Maddie picked out a spot where she could see him but not be too obvious. Reaching into her duffle bag, she pulled out the large beach towel and then dumped the rest of her stuff onto the towel. She picked up her Kindle, sat down, and powered it up. She tried to focus on the words in front of her, but kept getting distracted.

He is kind of hot, she thought. Girls kept approaching his stand trying to talk to him, but he ignored them, never letting his eyes leave the water. *He knows what's important.* Maddie liked the way he used lack of eye contact to ward off the girls vying for his attention. She smiled and wondered whether any of these admirers had witnessed his chicken wings. Probably not.

He stood up to stretch and glanced around. His eyes landed on hers, and his face broke into the same brilliant smile she had seen during their run. She smiled back and returned his subtle wave. *OK,* she thought, *that wasn't so bad.* She considered going over, but then he turned and sat down again. *So much for that.*

Maddie had worked as a lifeguard in high school, and the training had stayed with her. She couldn't help scanning the water in zigzag patterns. She knew it was silly, but her knowledge of the water held her accountable. While she watched, she attempted to quiet her parents' voices. You need friends. You should go out. You should be having fun. She realized she didn't have many fun things in her life. And those hummingbirds. . . . OK, she thought, *maybe they do have a point.*

Shaking her head to exorcise the voices, she went back to scanning the water. There was a huge family group camped three spots over and a few rows closer to the water. Maddie found herself wondering what it would be like to be raised in such a large household. She was an only child and believed it was the sole reason so much energy was directed at her upbringing. Perhaps if she'd had siblings, her parents would have spread the attention among them. She tried to count the number of children in the family near her and settled on nine. Nine children. Maybe a couple of them were tag-along friends, but still, how can you keep your eye on that many kids?

"Jack, stop putting the dry ones on top. You're ruining it. Mom!" An older brother was trying—rather unsuccessfully—to teach one of the youngest boys to build a sandcastle.

"I'm reading a book to Josie; you'll have to solve it yourselves," the mother called back. An infant was perched in her lap under the umbrella.

The oldest—a girl about fourteen—was in the water with a baby on her hip, two toddlers sitting on the sand with waves brushing their sandy little feet clean, and two grade-schoolers on boogie boards floating close by.

"Bobby, come a little closer. Mom said you can't go out so far," the girl called out to the little boy in the water. Maddie concluded that parents like this probably let their kids stretch and be independent, unlike her parents. Dad scooped up the sandcastle builder and plopped him on the blanket with Mom. Taking the oldest boy with him, he headed toward the boardwalk.

She went back into lifeguard mode, scanning back and forth. Yesterday's storm had brought in some pretty big rollers that encouraged the kids to play "jump the waves." Their delightful squeals made Maddie smile. Crowds of people collected along the water's edge, creating a rainbow of colors: turquoise bikinis, red-yellow-blue beach balls, lime-green sand buckets, and cherry-red swim trunks.

Thinking of red swim trunks, Maddie allowed her gaze to land on the lifeguard again. He was hard at work but had added the stereotypical white stripe of zinc down the bridge of his nose. This time, she did laugh. He pointed at her—and then back to himself—and yelled out, "You laughing at me?" He smiled and held up the tube of zinc. "Want some?" Maddie laughed again and shook her head.

The dad was back with armloads of boardwalk food. The older boy arranged all the spoils on the second unoccupied blanket, while his dad went down to the water to round up the troops. The teenaged girl turned and yelled at two boogie-boarders, "Come in. Time for lunch."

Maddie's stomach growled. She reached for a bag of cocoa almonds, poured a handful into her mouth, and started chewing them begrudgingly, wishing for a slice of pizza instead. Eyes back on the sand, she saw the gaggle of kids coming up for their lunch. Mentally counting the bunch, she came up one short.

There, in the water, a little girl in a frilly pink-and-white bikini was still floating on her board. It looked like she was going farther out instead of coming in, a bit unsteady after the last roller. Turning to the beach, her little hands had a death grip on the side of her board, and she was yelling for her sister. She drifted farther away, into the middle of some breakers. At least twenty feet separated the girl from where she was moments before. When the breaker passed, Maddie didn't see the pink bikini where it was supposed to be. Instead, she saw an empty boogie board, floating toward the shore on what remained of the wave.

Maddie stood to get a better look. The boogie board was bobbing against the sand. No sign of its owner. She looked over at the lifeguard, but his eyes were down beach. She glanced back at the family. Pink bikini must be among them, noshing on some Thrasher's fries. That's how it's supposed to be—except, she wasn't there. Maddie heard her mother's voice, "Go, Maddie, it's all you. Go!" She raced toward the water with her eyes focused on the child's last point of air.

All her years of training resurfaced quickly. Adrenaline coursing through her powerful legs, Maddie swooped up the abandoned boogie board, whisked it under her arm, and plunged into the water toward the spot where she had last seen the frightened child. She was up to her neck, but there was no sign of the girl. Waves were coming in at a good clip, but ten seconds later, still no girl. Maddie dove under, her arms seeking to connect with a limb. Breaking through the surf for a fresh breath, Maddie spotted the child as she popped up just out of reach. Choking furiously, the girl looked at Maddie with terrified eyes and went under again.

Two more lunges, and Maddie was able to grab the tiny girl. Hauling her limp body to the surface, Maddie pushed the boogie board underneath, yanked the girl on top, and pulled her toward the beach. "I've got you," Maddie said calmly. "You're gonna be just fine now. Everything's OK."

Foamy water ran from the girl's mouth. Maddie tipped her on her side to help clear the saltwater from her airway, reassuring her while moving as fast as she could toward the beach.

The child seemed to come to life, let out a panicked wail, and grabbed for Maddie, who was suddenly aware of splashing and commotion nearby. She turned and realized that Chicken Wings had responded and was right beside her. Together, they pulled the boogie board toward shore, making sure the girl was still able to breathe.

One of the other lifeguards shouted that an ambulance was en route. Maddie spotted the little girl's parents standing in the water, frozen with fear. Hand clasped over her mouth, the mother was already crying. The father tried to get to his daughter.

"Sir, please step back," warned the lifeguard.

"It's my daughter—Jessie, Jessie!" he shouted.

"Sir, step back and let us do our job; let us help her."

The sound of a siren lent an air of authority to his demand. When the dad saw the approaching ambulance, he quickly stepped back next to his wife, and they watched with desperate hope in their eyes.

Chicken Wings, with Maddie's help, pulled the child off the board and turned her on her side again. The white foam seemed endless, and the child appeared barely conscious. She had been slammed into the ocean floor hard enough to take off several layers of skin. The areas that had come into contact with the abrasive sand were now bleeding and raw. The response team arrived and briskly pushed their way through the crowd. They lifted the girl onto a stretcher and hustled her into the ambulance.

Chicken Wings, who, thanks to the EMT driver, Maddie now knew as Todd, quickly wrapped his arm around the girl's mother and ushered her inside the ambulance with her child. Then he jogged over to Jessie's dad and Maddie. "She's going to be fine. Don't worry."

Jessie's dad grabbed Todd's hand and enthusiastically pumped it up and down in a firm handshake. "Thank you so much. You saved her. Thank you."

"Actually, this is the person who saved her." Todd turned to Maddie. "It was all you."

Maddie's cheeks brightened. "It was a team effort," she choked in reply.

Maddie helped the rest of the family pack up quickly while Todd gave Jessie's dad directions to the hospital. Before leaving, Jessie's father came over and put an arm around Maddie. "You have no idea how thankful we are." His face was contorted with anguish. "I don't have enough words." Grateful tears wet his face as he got into the car to head for the hospital.

Todd walked beside her on her way over to her blanket. "Wow, that was pretty intense, huh? By the way, I've never seen anyone move as fast as you did. You were amazing."

Maddie laughed, "You were right behind me, so I guess we're both pretty spectacular. By the way, I'm Maddie."

"Awesome. I'm Todd. You live around here?"

"Nope, just here on break. I'm staying at the Sea Sprite over on Olive." Maddie reached down to grab her bag, stuffing the scattered items back into it. Standing, she turned toward Todd. His eyes were fixed on her duffle bag.

"Hey—no way. You go to UVA?"

She pulled her bag in front of her and glanced down at the logo on the side of it. "Yeah, sure do." She smiled.

"So cool. I'm starting there in the fall. Maybe you could be my guide. Do you know anyone on the swim team?"

"Actually, I'm on the swim team," she said with a smile.

"Well, that explains a lot. Dang, I knocked it out of the park without even trying." They both laughed. "Listen, a bunch of us are getting together tonight for some pizza. Wanna join?"

"Well ... I'm, uh. . . ."

"Tell you what. I'll stop by after work, and we can walk over together. How's that? And if you want, I can bring Tina and Rachel. They lifeguard with me. They're both going to UVA, too. I know they'd want to meet you. None of us can stay late because we have to be up early for workouts, but it'll be great to hang for a while."

❧

Maddie walked back to the Sea Sprite with quite a different attitude than the one she'd had when she left. She described her day to Jillian as she sat at the counter eating some freshly cut pineapple chunks.

"Holy cow, girl. That's unbelievable. You saved a little girl's life? Come here." Jillian rushed the stool Maddie was perched on and almost knocked her down trying to give her a hug. Maddie hadn't thought of her actions as heroic, but here was Jillian, celebrating her efforts. Maybe it was worthy of a spin or two in the kitchen, but it didn't stop Maddie from being a little embarrassed by the attention.

"Thanks. I ... uh ... only have a little time to change and

get ready before they get here, so I better. . . ."

"Of course," said Jillian. "Go get yourself ready. Hurry. Scoot."

Todd showed up twenty minutes early with his two friends.

"Hey, Maddie, these are the friends I told you about who are going to UVA." He turned toward the lanky blonde and said, "This is Tina. She's in cross-country, and she's gonna be an engineer, but not with trains—with plastic stuff." He turned from Tina to a petite, black-haired beauty and continued, "And this is Rachel. She's on my swim team and wants to swim at UVA, too. She's going to work on people's feet." The group all laughed at his descriptive skills.

"Todd's our heeerrrooo," teased Tina, sidling up to Todd and batting her eyelashes.

"Uh huh. The hero who only showed up in time to get the pretty girl's number," Rachel added, laughing.

"So," said Tina to Maddie, "you're the talk of the beach today. It was nice of you to help lifeguard Todd here save that little girl. I saw him staring at you while I was on break, so I'm surprised he even noticed a drowning girl."

Todd's cheeks turned red. Rachel jumped into the mix, "Yeah, I'm thinking he should sign his paycheck over to Maddie here since she's the one who earned it." The laughter started again.

Todd blushed and chuckled, "Well, I did help get her to the beach *and* helped them get her into the ambulance, *and* I also filled out the paperwork."

"Yup, we all know Maddie gets the credit for the save," said Tina. "Of course, we really do have to give him kudos for picking a real girl instead of a lifeguard groupie. Now we know why he's been holding out."

Jillian walked in and, hearing the last exchange, hooted in agreement. "Hey, since you guys are early, why don't you help yourselves to some cookies and lemonade before you head out?" She gestured toward a tray in the reception area that was loaded up with goodies.

The trio wandered around, politely commenting on the antique furnishings. Todd mentioned his parents were into "all this old stuff" and then spotted the items in the jewelry display case. "Wow. What's all this?"

Jillian laughed. "It's actually quite a mystery." Eagerly, the girls stepped over to the case to get a better look.

"About a year ago, I was doing a renovation project upstairs. My contractor stepped on a board in the floor and one end popped up. When he lifted the board out, the metal box you see there? It was underneath the floorboard. It's actually an ammo box from World War II. When we opened it, these things were inside, wrapped in a woman's scarf."

"Wow," Rachel said.

"Cool, right? My grandparents have owned this place for over fifty years, but the things you are looking at seem to date back to the 1930s and '40s."

"Who put them there?" Maddie asked.

"That's what I'm trying to find out," said Jillian.

They watched as Jillian pulled out the items one by one: A black-and-white photograph, a tube of lipstick, a tiny silver purse, a locket, a small glass vial filled with sand and sealed with cork, a harmonica, a pin, and a pair of torn movie tickets.

"This is so cool," said Tina, opening the lipstick container. "It's still got lipstick in it."

"Umm, this lady?" Todd pointed at the photo. "I've seen her before, or at least a picture of her." He jumped when Jillian overenthusiastically grabbed his arm.

"This lady? Are you sure? You've seen this lady?"

"Yes. At least I think so."

"Todd, this is *huge*." Jillian's face broke into a wide grin that highlighted the laugh lines around her sparkling eyes. "It could help me figure out who owned the box. Do you remember where you saw her?" She was practically pleading.

"Whoa, cool. Yeah, I think I've seen her picture hanging up at my church."

"Where's your church?"

"Right across the street. All Saints."

Jillian grabbed both of his hands and started jumping up and down.

"That's awesome."

Now the girls, Todd, and Maddie were all laughing.

"OK, you kids go have fun," Jillian said, almost pushing them out of the Sea Sprite. "I'm going to call the church to see if I can find out anything." She started back toward her desk and then turned her head back to Todd and said, "Thank you so, so, much."

"No problem; I hope it helps."

Maddie and Todd walked alone, and the girls ran ahead to grab a table for pizza.

After they finished, Todd offered to walk Maddie back to the Sea Sprite.

"Thanks so much for inviting me and for introducing me to Tina and Rachel," said Maddie. "They're nice."

"Yeah, it was really fun. The whole day's been pretty great."

"No kidding. I'm probably not even going to be able to sleep tonight, I'm so wired."

"Me, too, and that's bad because I have to be on the beach at seven tomorrow morning for mandatory workouts."

All too soon, they were back at the inn. As Maddie turned toward the walk, Todd reached for her hands. I'm having a hard time figuring out if I'm so psyched because of the rescue, because I'm going to UVA, or because I met you."

"Maybe it's a combo deal," Maddie said with a smile.

"Yeah, or maybe," he said, "it's because even after the summer is over, I'll get to see you." He squeezed her hands in his.

This time when he smiled, Maddie only saw his bright teeth. She thought for a minute and chuckled to herself. *Actually, I've always kind of liked chicken wings.*

"But summer isn't quite over, so I'm hoping to see you tomorrow—without Tina and Rachel," he said as he started back down the street.

Maddie yelled an "OK" and waved.

She watched until he turned the corner. Then she spun around and skipped her way up the steps. As she closed the door of the Sea Sprite behind her, she whispered, "Yabba dabba doooo."

Jillian's Journal

June 6th

A real hero stayed here this week. Maddie actually saved a little girls life! I hope she carries that pride with her the rest of her life. Watching Maddie struggle with her parents reminds me of why I make the decisions I do. I need to be a good example for Maegan. I hope one day she understands. Maddie showed me that sticking to a goal and working toward it with passion is where the reward hides. It may not give you the win you think it will, but in the end, the win comes from the work. The Sea Sprite's reinvention is a great example.

My takeaways from this week?

One – I want to keep up the hard work. The reward may not be a million bucks in the bank, but whatever satisfaction I get through the work will be reward enough.

Two – Did the hummingbirds show up for Maddie or for me? Note to self: ask Greta for more info.

Oh! I almost forgot. I found her! Well, I didn't find her, Todd did. I am so glad the treasures are in the display case. I've learned a lot already, but I sure didn't expect my guests to help. The girl in my photo is the same one in the church picture Todd saw. In the church picture, she's standing next to the Reverend. On the back of the photo, someone wrote, "Helen, 15 yrs, with Reverend McGarry." Well, hello, Helen. Nice to meet you. Where are you hiding?

FERRY FIRST TIME

*T*he reservation line was ringing, the doorbell chiming, and the oven timer beeping. *All in a day's work*, thought Jillian, as she sprang toward the ringing phone to grab it on her way to the oven.

"Sea Sprite Inn, this is Jillian. Are you calling because you need to relax at the beach?" *Ugh. I don't like that opener, either.*

From the sound of it, the caller had a household as busy as her morning at the Sea Sprite. Jillian heard a toddler demanding attention, while the mom tried to forge a temporary alliance to allow enough time for a brief phone conversation. Then the woman's voice blurted out, "I'll call you right back. She's about to knock over. . . ."

Jillian heard a crash, and then the line went dead. She giggled as she set the phone down on the counter, grabbed the hot pads, and hoped for the best as she swung open the oven door. A blast of hot, moist cinnamon air hit her full on the face. She felt her eyebrows singe as she leaned in to retrieve the pecan-crusted sweet rolls. Setting the baking dish on the stove, she grabbed the phone and turned back down the hallway to answer the door, calling out, "Be right there."

The familiar brown UPS uniform was a welcome sight. She opened the door, apologized for the wait, and as she reached for the electronic signature pad, the phone in her pocket rang. She simultaneously handed off the signature pad, reached for her box, mouthed a "thank you" to the driver, and answered the phone.

"Sea Sprite Inn, this is Jillian. Are you calling because you need to relax at the beach?" *Yep, still awkward.*

"Hi. I'm sorry. I just called but then had to hang up. My name's Beth. I'm trying to make a reservation for the second week of June for three of us: my husband, Steve, our energetic four-year-old daughter, Chloe, and myself. It's a little last minute, but I'm hoping you have an opening for our frazzled little family?" Beth ended with a deep sigh, punctuated by squeals in the background.

"Sure. We can make that work," said Jillian.

"Fantastic. Let me grab my wallet and take care of the reservation right now. Can you hold on for a second?"

"Of course."

Jillian perked up at the thought of hosting a wee one. Lots of bed and breakfast owners offered rooms only to adults and children twelve and up, but Jillian loved kids and missed the cheerful giggles. The baby voice of her now-grown daughter, Maegan, had been silent for so many years, it almost seemed impossible. With that in mind, she had decided to allow children of any age—at least for the first year.

"I'm so sorry to keep you waiting. I can't find my purse. Chloe was dragging it around earlier during her dress-up performance. It's probably lost in the pile of Disney princess gowns. Would it be all right if my husband calls later to pay the deposit?"

"Sure. I'll hold the room for forty-eight hours. Are there

any special arrangements, accommodations, or activities I can help you with?"

Beth hesitated before answering. "I should let you in on the secret. I just found out officially a few days ago that we're expecting another baby. I'd like to tell Steve during the vacation, instead of in the middle of a busy work week. If you could help me arrange some private time, it would be great. It means we'll need a babysitter for Chloe. Maybe you have some recommendations?"

"Congratulations—how exciting! There are definitely places for a romantic night for the two of you, and I do have options for sitters."

"Thank you so much. That would be a great help. To be honest, I'm feeling a little overwhelmed at the moment."

When the call ended, Jillian snickered to herself, remembering the days when Maegan was a baby and how chaotic each moment seemed. She wanted to make sure Beth's stay was everything she hoped for.

Friday, Beth's husband called to reserve the room, but only for Beth and Chloe.

"The thing is, we really needed this vacation away together, but I had a huge project dumped in my lap at work, and there's no way I can make it to the beach." His sadness was palpable, and it filtered through the phone line.

"Steve, do what you need to do. I'll take great care of them down here and make sure they have a terrific time. Count on it." Jillian couldn't help feeling sad for the little family and made up her mind she was going to try to make their visit as special as she could.

Discussing the need for family time had reminded Jillian that she needed some quiet time with Gramps. His perspective always grounded her and made her think. He usually answered her questions before she could even figure out how to ask them.

As soon as she exited the elevator on his floor, Jillian could hear him. His voice—a deep baritone—always carried, no matter how hard he tried to keep it down. Grandma used to try to quiet him when Jilly was upstairs in bed. "George darling," she would say, "your voice could wake Lazarus." He would answer: "My dear, loud is the way I live!" Then Jillian would hear them laughing. She loved to fall asleep listening to them laugh.

She heard him laughing now as she walked down the hall. She pictured his wide grin, the cleft in his chin, and lively eyes that were the color of maple syrup. Even without much more than a Friar Tuck smattering of hair around the outside of his head, he was a vital and handsome man. At ninety-one, his claim to fame was he still had all of his own teeth. He declared it was a direct result of exercising them by eating loads of beef jerky. Not any beef jerky. It has to be the "trucker kind," he would tell anyone who asked.

"Now listen here, you little troublemaker," Gramps was saying to the nurse. "You stop trying to get me to show my backside. I told you I wanted another gown to cover up with back there. I think you're trying to see it for free."

"Mr. Whittaker, you are too much, I swear," the nurse responded. Laughing on her way out of his room, she almost collided with Jillian.

"Hi, Gramps."

"My Jelly girl! Oh my. Come here, darlin'! It's so damn good to see you. You won't believe the stuff they're trying to pass off as food. Think you can sneak in some jerky for me?"

"I don't know if you're supposed to—"

"Aww, it figures. I can't get away with anything. So how's my girl?"

"Things are great with me. More importantly, how are you feeling?"

"Spill it, Jilly. I see wrinkles in your eyebrows. What's troubling you?"

She should have known he would be able to read her. Jillian had ignored the elephant in the room for too long herself. She hoped that if she didn't acknowledge its existence, it might disappear altogether. But that never happens, at least not when you want it to. She wanted to protect Maegan—and for that matter, Gramps, too—from the pain that would remain long after the dust settled.

"Gramps, Chad and I ... we're going through a pretty rough time right now." Her eyes searched his face for a reaction.

"What's going on?" he asked.

"He's ... well ... for one thing, he was having an affair."

His eyes lifted a bit. "Sorry, Jilly. Never did trust him. His mouth says one thing, but his eyes say another."

"Why didn't you say anything?"

"Jilly, you'll figure it out. You know you're better off staying clear of him. I'm sorry it hurts, but don't forget what I've always said. You become who you hang around. The rules are the same now as they were when you were growing up."

"I was scared to tell you. He said it would kill you and ruin Maegan. He said I wouldn't make it without him."

Jillian's voice quieted.

"People like him, Jilly, they'll tell you they are the best thing that ever happened to you. Truth is, they're the ones who need you. I've seen it a hundred times. You're in charge of how you spend your time and whether or not you're happy doing it. You need to decide what kind of future you want and who you want to be. Then do it. Simple as that. Do yourself a favor; don't make it any more complicated."

Jillian sat down on the bed next to Gramps and leaned in. She relaxed and gave up the battle of trying to hold herself together. Melting into his hug, she felt her worries lift a little, like they always did when she was with him.

Beth parked the car behind the Sea Sprite. The last two hours in the car were silent, giving her time to contemplate the changes that were coming. She sat for a moment, relishing the quiet. Although she loved her daughter more than anything, Chloe was quite a handful and had learned early how easy it was to push her buttons. Beth peeked at her over the headrest. A crown of glossy, brown bangs framed softly arched brows. The slope of Chloe's nose led to lips that gently parted with each soft, little-girl snore. Her little "mini me." Ever since Chloe was born, Beth had heard the line, "She looks *exactly* like you." Beth shook her head, thinking, *With the exception of our features, this child is* nothing *like me.*

For the hundredth time today, Beth's brow furrowed under her own brown bangs, and she felt a wave of fear wash over her. She should consider herself lucky to have a wonderful husband and daughter, but she wasn't feeling fortunate. Lately, she felt alone. Afraid, alone, overwhelmed, and unappreciated. *Steve and I used to tackle everything as a team. We both had great careers, and duties at home were shared, totally shared. But lately, he's been spending so much time at work that running the house is all on me. Now he can't even join us on a little vacation. Will having another child be too much?*

Beth decided that, despite the change in plans, she would make the best of their time at the beach. If nothing else, she would enjoy the new scenery, and who knows, maybe this was the break she needed. She got out of the car and walked around to get Chloe out of her car seat. Chloe's eyes opened slowly and she smiled.

"Mama, are we there now? At vacation?"

"Yes, honey. We're at vacation."

Beth planted a big smooch on Chloe's cheek and watched her scramble out of the car. Beth grabbed the bags from the floor and handed the princess roller bag to Chloe. Hand in hand, the two walked through the back garden toward the rear porch of the Sea Sprite.

Someone had thoughtfully placed artistic stepping stones leading from the parking area to the inn. The stones—some with sparkling mermaids, fairies, or gnomes—led them through an opening in the hedgerow. At each side, huge arms of white jasmine and rambling rose were trained over a homemade arch of bamboo stalks, and Beth noticed strands of tiny lights twisted among the vines. Although the entrance was beautiful during the day, it would be absolutely stunning at night.

As they walked into the backyard, Chloe spotted a captivating little garden. Several of the trees sheltering the secluded area had tiny doors and windows attached to their base. Matching pieces of furniture built to an unbelievably small scale and miniscule bird baths were placed along little moss paths connecting several of the doors. Beyond this fairy village, there was a small—but human-sized—building with a roof of corrugated steel and walls made almost entirely of large antique windows. Both glass doors were propped open to the garden, and inside was an inviting floral couch, a rocker, and a small table with cushioned chairs. From its door hung a hand-painted sign that read, "The Nook Nest." *How lovely,* thought Beth. *This is where I'm spending any quiet time I get during this visit.*

Chloe and Beth explored the garden for a few more minutes, and then Beth said, "OK, Chloe, it's time to go check into our room. We'll come back down after we put our things away."

Chloe looked fascinated with the jewels and designs on the stepping stones. "I want to stay here."

"No, Chloe, come with me. I've already told you what we need to do first."

That was all it took. The outburst that followed was truly epic. "Noooooooooo!" Chloe plopped down onto the ground, crying uncontrollably. Beth tried to calm her daughter, but Chloe was having none of it. "I want my daddy," she yelled.

Yeah, me, too, thought Beth.

She left her daughter kicking in the dirt and rang the bell on the back porch. As the door opened, a heavenly aroma wafted out from the kitchen. A pretty woman with long, dark, wavy hair and bright eyes held the door open for her with a large, genuine smile. Her clothes were stylish and flattered her curvy frame.

"Hi, I'm Jillian."

"Jillian, it's great to meet you. I'm Beth. And the little girl kicking the ground is my daughter, Chloe."

Chloe stopped kicking and begrudgingly joined her mother. She whined, attempting to pull Beth's hand toward the yard again. "Mommmmm, I want to see the little houses."

Beth sighed and responded, "No, Chloe, I told you. We have to put our things in our room first. When we're done, I'll think about it."

"But Mom—"

"Tell you what, Chloe," said Jillian. "I'm thinking of having a scoop of orange sherbet. Would you like one?"

The unusually warm and humid June day was so stifling, even Chloe was softened by the offer.

"OK."

Jillian bent down until she was eye level with Chloe and gave her the once-over. "You're a little doll. Great shoes. Why, I'll bet you're wearing those cool shoes that light up when you walk, aren't you?"

"Yes," answered Chloe, "they *are* light-up shoes. They make me run fast, see?" Chloe picked up her feet and ran down the hallway. On her way back, her arm bumped a side table. Both Jillian and Beth waited for the table to tip over, but thankfully, it teetered and held its ground.

"My, you are a really fast runner," said Jillian.

"Chloe, no running in the house. I've already told you about inside rules." Beth's face flushed with embarrassment.

"Your mom is right, Chloe. There is no running inside. We have inside rules here, but you're a smart girl, so I bet you'll do your best to listen, won't you?"

The child hesitated and then stammered, "Yes."

"Great," Jillian responded, "because you want me to tell everyone here you're a big girl. And only big girls get ice cream and treats." She talked as she scooped out a small ball of sherbet and placed it in a bowl for Chloe. "Why don't you sit over here at the kitchen table where you can see the garden?"

Beth could tell by the interaction that Jillian was already captivated by Chloe, and miraculously, Jillian had managed to capture Chloe's attention. Beth relaxed onto a stool at the counter in the large, welcoming kitchen. She watched as Chloe gazed at the multicolored glass globes glistening from their hooks in front of the large windows and busily scooped the orange treat into her mouth.

Jillian pulled out a stool for herself. "How was the drive down from Jersey?"

"Terrible. I couldn't believe the backup near the Christiana Mall. It must have taken me an extra forty minutes to navigate through that mess."

"Oh my," said Jillian. "I should've thought to tell you to go through Cape May. You drive south to Cape May and there's a ferry that carries you across. In fact, the ferry ride would be a nice day trip for you and Chloe."

"Sounds like a lot of fun. Maybe we can do it Wednesday. The weather is supposed to be cooler and gorgeous."

"I want to see the ferry, Mom. Please? Please can we go? Can we go now? Pleeeaaasseee?"

"Chloe, we'll go, but not today. I'll tell you when I decide."

Chloe began to launch into a full meltdown.

"Oh my. I'm afraid you may not be able to get on the ferry after all." Jillian sighed.

"Why not?" said Chloe, thrown off-kilter by the calmly

delivered comment in the middle of her outburst.

"Because they only allow big girls who wait their turn and finish their chores. Baby girls who throw temper tantrums aren't allowed because the loud noises scare people." Jillian turned and winked at Beth. "So are you a big girl? Or a baby girl?"

"I'm a big girl."

"Well, you'll have to show me. Big girls bring their dirty ice cream dishes to the sink." Chloe's shoes lit up as she scampered to retrieve the bowl.

"And they put their clothes away, too," added Beth.

"You're right, they sure do. I better get you two upstairs to show you around."

⚷

Beth and Chloe followed Jillian up to the Sandcastle Room. The moment she saw it, Beth was thrilled with the choice. The off-white furniture stood out in soft contrast against the pale peach walls. A chandelier—hung in the middle of the ceiling—threw its sparkled light over the entire room. Brushed-gold lamps anchored each side of the bed, and a gilded painting of a golden crown reflected the lights. Against the far wall, a painting of a huge sandcastle hung over a fluffy sofa. Chloe immediately spotted the upholstered gliding rocker and climbed up into it.

Beth smiled. "This is a gorgeous room. It's so peaceful and pretty."

Jillian opened a side door to reveal a short, wide hall containing a closet with built-in drawers on the left and a half bath on the right. "The spa room is through here." Jillian opened a door at the end of the hall. "You and Chloe will be sharing it with another family."

Beth couldn't contain her excitement. "Oh my gosh. What an incredible shower. I can't wait to use this," she said, taking in the huge walk-in shower with four body jets, a rainhead, and two hand-held shower wands. "Or maybe I'll unwind in a tub full of bubbles," she said, spotting the soaker tub. "Tough decision." With a huge smile on her face, she walked right into the shower stall. Chloe followed, laughing at her mother.

"Yes," said Jillian. "I admit I went a little overboard with this room, but it's so relaxing and, well, spa-like," she said.

"You nailed it," said Beth.

Nobody had noticed Chloe's pudgy little hands gripping the shower control, and suddenly cold water shot out, spraying both Beth and Chloe. Jillian quickly turned off the tap and gave Beth two fluffy white towels. "Looks like the decision was made for you," Jillian said with a smile.

As they returned to the Sandcastle Room, Jillian handed Beth a Sea Sprite schedule and amenities booklet and excused herself so her new guests could settle in.

After they had dried off and unpacked, Beth and Chloe went downstairs to explore the Sea Sprite and its grounds. Beth learned the Richards family was booked for the same week, and their family included twins, Emily and Olivia, who were ten, and older sister Hannah, who was thirteen. Chloe would enjoy having some older girls around.

After a walk around the yard, Beth curled up with a novel on the outdoor sofa in the Nook Nest, while Chloe happily played in the garden. The Richards twins waved from their sundeck. When Chloe called, "Come down and see the fairy village," both girls scampered outside to play. The day passed with great speed and an equal measure of quiet. Beth decided she could easily get used to life at the

Sea Sprite, especially if she could look forward to the use of the spa room every day.

⚷

Monday morning found Beth unable to get out of bed. Each time she sat up, the burning in her throat started, and new waves of nausea began. She asked Chloe to see if there were any crackers downstairs. Chloe returned with Jillian, who carried a tray with a can of Vernor's ginger ale, some Saltines, and a banana. Jillian suggested Chloe go downstairs and sit with the Richards girls in the dining room.

When she had gone, Jillian said, "Looks like morning sickness—am I right?"

"Yep, and great timing."

"Anything else I can do for you, just ask."

"Well, since you offered ... any chance you could speak with Mrs. Richards about the possibility of Hannah babysitting for the day?"

"Sure. No problem."

"And you mentioned the ferry and the Cape May Zoo. I want to make sure we get there on Wednesday. Could I ask you to make the arrangements for us?"

Jillian smiled. "Of course."

Beth started to get up to grab her purse for the credit card. Her hand clamped over her mouth. *Deep breaths.* She glanced apologetically at Jillian.

"Sorry. Guess it'll have to wait."

"No worries. You need some rest. I'm sure you'll be up and about in no time. I'll go down and keep an eye on Princess Chloe until you feel up to joining us."

The moment Beth heard the door click shut, she sighed with relief. *Just a few minutes of quiet.*

Downstairs, quiet was nowhere to be found. All four girls were helping themselves to the snacks and busily planning their day. Emily, Olivia, and Hannah bounced around the dining room, babbling about the waterslide at Jungle Jim's and how they were going to float in the lazy river on inner tubes. Chloe piped up, "This is gonna be so *fun*. I can't wait."

"Chloe, honey," Jillian began gently, "you may need to check with your mom first. Looks like she's not feeling well and may not be able to take you."

Chloe's face crumpled and she began to wail. Hannah, Olivia, and Emily looked at her in shock.

Hannah was first to talk. "Chloe—knock it off. Why are you being such a baby? Geez."

Emily and Olivia simultaneously said, "It's nothing to cry about," and "What a baby," and although Chloe couldn't tell which girl had said what, she instantly stopped crying to defend herself.

"I'm not a baby."

"Then why are you acting like one?" asked Hannah.

"I want to go, too."

"But you can't go if you're gonna be a crybaby."

Chloe's eyes lifted. "OK. Can I go if I promise I won't be a baby?"

"Maybe, if you pinky-swear with us," commanded Hannah, extending her finger. Olivia and Emily quickly put their tiny fingers into the mix. Chloe was wide-eyed and looked puzzled.

"Chloe, take your pinky and wrap it around ours," said

Hannah. "Then say, 'I swear and promise I will not be a baby anymore,' and I'll ask my mom and dad if you can go with us."

Chloe solemnly complied.

Jillian heard the exchange in the front hall and took Mrs. Richards aside to offer an idea. "You know, Denise," she said, "Chloe's mom isn't feeling well, and she asked if Hannah might be able to babysit Chloe today. Do you think she would be willing to watch Chloe at Jungle Jim's?"

Within minutes of hearing the plan, Beth doled out quick approval and plenty of spending money. The gang loudly and joyously funneled out of the Sea Sprite for their day at the waterpark.

Jillian sat down at her desk and took a deep breath. She checked the little notebook she carried with her to make sure her tasks were checked off. Sometimes, the day got away from her. This notebook had saved her on more than one occasion. Today, the only thing unfinished was making reservations for Beth and Chloe's ferry ride for Wednesday. As she pulled up the Cape May-Lewes Ferry website and started to fill in the information for their reservation, the phone rang. The familiar voice surprised Jillian. She was thrilled to hear about the change in plans and to be part of a secret surprise. She helped the caller with the special details he requested for his visit. Life was good at the Sea Sprite.

Beth woke early on Wednesday. Thankfully, she felt considerably better and was able to shower and dress before waking Chloe.

"Chloe," she whispered. "Chloe, it's time for the ferry ride, sleepyhead."

Chloe slowly opened her eyes. "It *is*?" And as the words sunk in, she became more animated. "It is?" Beth nodded. "Yay! It's today." Chloe bounded out of bed and eagerly pulled out her clothes, dragging them back to the bed to start dressing.

Beth noted that Chloe seemed to be between stages, but increasingly she acted like a "big girl," giving Beth more confidence. Maybe she *would* have enough energy for a second child. Then, just as swiftly, she caught herself with dark thoughts about how she would still need to do it all alone. She and Chloe went downstairs to grab a few snacks for the ride and headed for the ferry terminal.

Beth drove the car onto the ferry and parked. She and Chloe walked to the boat's upper deck and sat outside to watch the water. They were both startled as the ferry sounded its horns and the engines growled to life. As the noise increased in volume, the ferry began moving toward Cape May. Morning sun lit the crowded deck.

A silver-haired couple sat two seats away. Beth wondered what their life was like together. *How many children had they raised? Did they do it together?* They looked happy, sitting with their legs touching and their heads leaning toward each other while they smiled and talked. *That's what I want. Years from now, I want us to be—just there for each other.*

The crosswinds increased as the ferry picked up speed. Chloe and Beth laughed at their wild, crazy hairstyles that changed every second or two with the breeze. The silver couple noticed them laughing, and smiled.

"You're such a pretty little girl," the woman said to Chloe.

"Thank you," Chloe answered politely, and Beth breathed a little sigh of relief.

"Is this your first ride on the ferry?"

"Not yet. But I can today because I've been a big girl."

"But you are on the ferry, sweetheart. Isn't it fun?"

Chloe's face scrunched up. "Mom, when will we be on the ride?"

"This *is* the ride, Chloe. It's taking us and our car across the water."

"No, Mom. You promised." Chloe looked like she was barely keeping her composure.

"Chloe, I promised you a ferry ride. This *is* the ferry ride. What's the matter? You seem upset."

Chloe took a deep breath. "Mom, this is *not* a fairy. This is a boat, not a fairy. You promised I can ride the fairy."

Beth looked at Chloe so stunned, she didn't respond immediately.

The silver couple was listening to the exchange. The gentleman was the first to fully comprehend the miscommunication. "Oh dear." He scooted closer to Chloe. "I think I know what happened here."

Chloe looked at him, waiting for an explanation.

"Now listen closely. I don't want you to miss what I'm going to say, OK?" Chloe nodded. "This *is* the fairy ride, but fairies are too tiny to carry us all on their little wings, so the boat is what carries us."

"Right," exclaimed Chloe. "Fairies do have wings."

Beth's brain began to catch up. She was thankful this wonderful man had filled in during her lapse. She stayed quiet while he continued his explanation.

"But the fairies are flying all around us, and they aren't

allowed to let us see them. Sometimes they put on special shows for the people on the boat. But you have to be patient and quiet. Do you want to look for the fairy show?"

"Yes," Chloe whispered.

"Come over here toward the railing then and look out at the water," he said, taking her hand.

Chloe scanned the water. "There," she said, pointing at an area where the sunlight twinkled on the tips of the waves, creating a shimmer. "Is that the fairy show?" She looked up at the man for confirmation.

"It sure is," he answered.

"Mom!" Chloe called out. "Come see them; the fairies are here for us."

Beth rose enthusiastically, but a wave of boat-inspired nausea gripped her, slowing her down. As she lumbered to the railing beside Chloe, a pair of dolphins jumped clear of the water only a few feet from the side of the boat. They broke through the water, only to dip back in with a graceful dive. The splash sent a sparkling shower of ocean water high into the air. Chloe squealed with delight.

The older man continued talking to Chloe while she watched for more dolphins. "Now you know the secret. If you keep your eye out, sometimes you will find special gifts the fairies bring especially for you. You have to keep looking." Chloe nodded earnestly.

"Thank you so much," said Beth. "You saved the day."

"After five kids," he said with a laugh, "we're old pros. Distraction and a little creativity can go a long way."

Well, Beth thought gratefully, *Chloe's not the only one who learned a new secret today.*

The ferry was close to docking in Cape May, and passengers had started to migrate to their vehicles on the first level. Beth took Chloe by the hand, bid the older couple good-bye, and tromped down the stairway to join the rail watchers on the lower level. Chloe was still mesmerized, watching for more of the fairy show in the water. Beth was more interested in observing the docking process to see what she could anticipate before the exit gate was dropped.

Something caught her attention to the left of the ramp. A solitary man stood by the rails near the dock area. He waved his arms frantically over his head. In one hand was a huge bouquet of daisies. *Well, someone is certainly getting a big welcome,* Beth thought.

She turned away to watch the gate drop, but several times the wind carried the sound of the man's yell. Wanting to see how it played out, Beth turned back to look. This time, the ferry was closer, and even Chloe noticed the man jumping on the dock.

It can't be. Recognition crept into Beth's brain as the space between them narrowed. His eyes locked with hers.

"Daddy!" screamed Chloe. "It's Daddy. The fairies brought Daddy, too."

It would seem so.

Smiling back at him, both Chloe and Beth waved wildly and then hurried to the car.

After exiting the ferry, Beth pulled into the parking lot, where she spotted Steve. As soon as Chloe was unbuckled, she ran to her daddy. Beth caught up—a bit out of breath—and hugged him tightly.

"Hey! How in the world did you know we were here?"

"A little bluebird told me you might be here this morning."

"A bird? Did the fairies bring you, Daddy?" asked Chloe.

"That's right," he answered.

Steve told Beth about his phone call with Jillian.

"What about the project?" she asked.

"I finished early and figured we could at least finish our vacation together."

Beth threw her arms around his neck with joy, and before long, they were back on the "fairy ride" back to Lewes.

Beth's rumbling stomach woke her at five thirty the next morning. She tried to remain in bed, but she was starving. She wandered downstairs and tip-toed to the front room, relieved to find some snacks on top of the glass case in the reception area. As she stuffed a handful of Cheez-Its into her mouth, she moved the snack containers to the side and studied the contents of the case.

The silk scarf caught her attention. It reminded Beth of her mom, who used to tie her hair back and wrap it in a scarf similar to this one. Beth wondered whether her mother had ever felt overwhelmed. Had she ever doubted she could handle their family? The picture next to the scarf showed young lovers on the beach, looking as if they were about to kiss. *They look so in love,* Beth thought. *I wonder if they lasted a lifetime?* She often felt more like Steve's business partner than his wife. *Is this what the vows meant by "for better or worse"? This is worse, right?*

The items in the case were an odd collection of old trinkets. She made a mental note to ask Jillian about them. Beth's focus was broken when she felt a pair of strong arms circle her waist from behind.

"Hey," Steve whispered. "I reached for you, but you weren't there."

The words should have comforted Beth, but didn't. They seemed to echo, waiting for a response. *I've been thinking the same thing—for years now.* She kept her thoughts tucked deeply inside, sighed, and chose to lean back against him instead.

"Come back to bed with me." He took her hand and led her up the stairs to the Sandcastle Room.

Later, Steve told Beth he had made plans for a private dinner. "It'll just be the two of us. Right here at the inn, but with our own chef."

Beth's eyes crinkled with pleasure at the thought. "What about Chloe?"

"It's all taken care of."

Jillian came around the corner and caught the tail end of the conversation. "I'm taking the night off, too. I hardly *ever* get the chance to enjoy boardwalk food, and tonight's the night. Chloe and I are going to hit Funland and eat at every boardwalk food stop." She laughed, patting the slight bulge around her tummy. "We'll be lucky if we can roll out of bed tomorrow."

So, thought Beth, *it was set.* She still hadn't finalized her script and had no idea how she was going to tell Steve what was on her mind and in her heart. Somehow, she hoped the right words would find their way.

After Steve and Beth had issued their last enthusiastic good-byes to Jillian and Chloe, they turned to each other and sighed. It was their turn. Steve offered his arm to Beth, and they sat on the verandah of the Sea Sprite. Both were warned not to trudge through the kitchen while Hari

Cameron, a local celebrity chef, was working on their private menu. Judging by the smells emanating from the back of the house, they were in for a wonderful evening. No elaborate preparations were needed for the two of them, so they sat together without much comment. It was enough just to—*be*. Beth turned and Steve leaned in for a kiss.

"Do you know how beautiful you are, Beth?"

She remained silent, but a small smile escaped.

"You light everything and make my world so much better."

He leaned in again to brush his lips against hers, whispering, "I love you."

She said it back but felt guilty for her lack of enthusiasm.

"So our CEO was really impressed with the package I presented. After the discussion, he made me an offer." His chest puffed up and he sat straighter. He paused briefly before continuing with excitement, "They're opening a satellite office, and he wants me to be the site manager. No more two-hour commute. It's ten minutes tops—door to door—and the hours are eight to five. Life's going to be normal again, babe."

Beth tried to be happy. He rambled on about how he was going to spend his extra time at the local gym, start riding his mountain bike again, and really take advantage of the new location. Beth listened and nodded. She could feel a slow burn starting in her cheeks. "Steve, that's great news. I'm really glad you won't be so far away, and no more commute. It's great for you."

The porch lights went on and off twice. Steve said, "That's our cue."

The timing couldn't have been better, thought Beth, as

they maneuvered through the front yard in the dark. The tiny, twinkling lights in the rose arch guided them toward their dinner destination.

"Do you remember our song, Beth?" Steve said, stopping her. "I do."

He gently took her in his arms, dancing with her slowly in a circle, singing softly, "Whenever I'm alone with you, you make me feel like I am whole again." Somehow, his grip felt tighter on her. She relaxed into it, letting herself feel protected.

They finished their walk over the bejeweled stepping stones and moved to the Nook Nest. Soft lights— meticulously hung—almost covered the windows from the outside. The little bulbs reflected through the glass and lit the inside of the structure. The only additional light was from a trio of simple candles flickering on the table, which was dressed in linen and burlap. Two heavily padded chairs, covered in gray satin, sat on either side. Steve pulled out a chair for Beth, and she sank into its welcoming cushion. He reached for the bottle of wine and filled her glass. The kitchen door opened, and Steve took his seat as they watched the chef cross the rear yard holding two small plates.

First Course: Virginia Fluke – Ginger Cardamom – Oca Sorrel

The food belonged on a magazine cover, and both Steve and Beth marveled over the unique combination of flavors. Steve was the first to mention how wonderful it was to be alone. Beth agreed, trying to remember the last time it happened. It was so long ago, she gave up. Instead, she tried to soak in all of the preparation he put into this night. She focused on how much he must love her to have planned all this.

"Beth, is something wrong? You don't like the wine?"

OK, this is it. "I'm sure the wine is great, but I don't think I should be drinking any." Beth paused dramatically to see how long it would take for him to register the meaning.

As the chef crossed the yard with the second course, he got it. Jumping up from the table, Steve yelled, "We're having a baby?"

Beth nodded and smiled. "We're having a baby."

He ran around the table and knelt in front of Beth's chair, wrapping his arms around her. Chef Hari smiled as he set the plates in front of their seats, bowed slightly, and then quietly left.

Second course: Berkshire Pork Cheek – Spinach – Cabbage – Green Apple

Steve kissed her and went back to his chair. Without taking the time to appreciate the pork cheek, he chomped and swallowed until his entree vanished, then turned back to Beth.

"Whatever it takes to make things easier on you, I'll do it. You know? I will. I promise."

"First of all," she began gently, "forget about joining the gym and mountain biking. There will be a time for that, but it's definitely not now. What I need is for you to figure out a way to give me at least one day of working from home each week."

"You've got it. Of course. I'll make it happen."

Suddenly, he seemed to spring to life. His childlike enthusiasm was one of the things Beth loved most about him.

"I can wake Chloe up every morning, feed her breakfast,

and walk her to day care."

"She would love that."

"And as soon as I get home, I'll take her to the park with the swings."

"Great idea." Beth tried to eat the food, but her body was warning against it. She pushed her plate toward her husband.

"Are you OK?"

"Yes," she said. "Just having a little trouble with my appetite. I think I need something sweet."

"I'll take care of it, right now." Steve enthusiastically ate her portion and took the empty plates to the chef. He returned with a promise something sweet was headed her way.

Within moments, Chef Hari was back.

Dessert: Shattered Lemon – Chamomile Gel – Habanero Honey

"I can teach Chloe how to ride bikes with me." Now Steve was practically oozing enthusiasm.

"She would be the best biking partner." Beth pictured them pedaling side by side, with Chloe on her pink Barbie bike with glitter handles.

"I'm sorry I've been so busy. It's going to be better. I promise. I'm here, I understand, and I love you so much."

Steve leaned over, embraced her in a powerful hug, and started planting wet smooches all over her face. When his slobbery lips reached her throat, she broke into laughter. Even after all of these years, he instinctively knew exactly how to make her laugh.

Their plates empty, Steve stood abruptly, jarring the

table slightly as he rose. He grabbed the wine bottle and poured each of them a small glass, then sat down and raised his glass for a toast. Beth slid the wine toward him and raised her water glass.

"I thought Moscato was your favorite?" Steve said.

"It is."

"Don't you want. . . . Oh God, I guess we don't want Ava to start drinking so early, right?"

Glowing, she answered, "You mean Owen?"

"Nah. I meant Cassidy."

"I'm sorry, I missed that. Did you say, Ethan?"

"No, I most certainly didn't. I said Cassidy."

Tears slid onto his laughing cheeks. He held Beth's face, kissing her deeply. "I love you so much."

She said it back. And meant it ... more than ever.

Jillian's Journal

June 27th

Wow. Plenty of kids this week. So far, I'm happy with my decision to allow them. Watching young mothers brings back so many memories. I saw Beth struggle with the reality she isn't Superwoman. I think all moms deal with this. We pour so much of ourselves into our families—until one day we realize we can't do it all. Being human, instead of trying to be superhuman, is also a valuable lesson for our children. We want them to ask for help if they need it, but we don't model the behavior. Teaching our kids it doesn't take teamwork, and one person can handle it all, makes them believe it's all good, because Mom does it all anyway. Wrong answer.

My takeaways?

One – It's like Gramps said, you have all the power. You're in charge of how you spend your time and whether or not you're happy doing it. You need to decide what kind of future you want and who you want to be. Then do it. Simple as that. Do yourself a favor; don't make it any more complicated.

Two – I'm glad tantrums are a thing of the past, but right now, I'm missing Maegan more than ever. Tonight she was thrilled to be getting ready for the Pamplona Bull Run. I'm not proud to say I had to coerce her to promise to stay out of the street. I think she only agreed when I told her how much I need her—her and a glass of Chardonnay. I may have kept the wine part my little secret.

THE MAGICAL SUIT

This may take longer than I thought. Even though it was the first year for The Sea Sprite Inn, Jillian had hoped for at least one guest a week, yet here she was facing a week with no bookings. She closed the calendar with a sigh. Then she realized she suddenly had some free time. *Maybe I'll pop by to see Amy.*

She and Amy had known each other for decades. When Jillian was nine years old, her parents were killed in a car accident, and Jillian was sent to live with her grandparents full-time. The budding fourth-grade bullies at school smelled her despair and found creative ways to torture her, but her new friend, Amy, always seemed to come to her rescue. They had been best friends ever since.

As usual, Jillian's wayward brown curls were sneaking out of their tight chignon. She had adopted the look when Robert Palmer's dancers were hot, and it was still her "go-to" style. Casually, she ran her hands over her favorite black shorts. They must have shrunk while hanging in her closet. Her "As Seen on TV" Wonder Button extended the waistline just enough to squeeze her little muffin top into them, but as she knocked on Amy and Greta's door, the Wonder Button popped off.

Amy's dog barked, and Jillian heard someone yell, "Come in."

Bending down, she picked up the traitorous button and walked in, struggling to put it back on so she wouldn't spend the morning trying to hold her pants together. Sir Richard sat loyally at her best friend's side, and they both watched Jillian's dilemma with great interest. When she walked past Amy, Jillian saw the dog stretch his neck as far as possible without leaving his post. He licked her shin in a cursory hello.

"Hello, Dick," said Jillian. She swiped his head with her hand. Dick—otherwise known as Sir Richard—was Amy's rescue mutt. Covered with a wiry rust and black coat spiked in crazy angles, the poor thing had one eye that was sewn shut, a second eye filled with cataracts, and one deaf ear, which resulted in him constantly cocking his head to one side as if he couldn't quite figure out what you were saying. Amy told everyone she named him after Sir Richard Branson because he was a little scruffy around the edges but lived a rich life.

Amy's girlfriend, Greta, sat next to her at the table, laughing. Greta was an artist and sold paintings of the quirky dog in her gallery. She could capture any character with a paintbrush. Jillian could always count on Greta laughing when she heard the dog called "Dick."

"Hey there," Amy said. "Coffee's ready when you are. Come join us. You know where everything is."

"Thanks." Jillian poured her mug almost full of cream and sugar, then topped if off with coffee. "You're kidding. You guys even have vegan coffee. Is that really a thing? Aren't the beans already vegan?"

"It's about the processing of the beans," said Amy. "And God, I'll never understand how you can drink it like that! It's like the first cup of coffee your mother ever ... oh ... sorry, Jilly."

"You don't have to apologize. Yes, it's exactly the way my mom made my first cup of coffee. Just so happens I never grew out of it." Jillian offered a soft smile. She sat down on the red retro chair at Amy's table.

"So what's up?" asked Amy.

"Looks like I'm free next week," Jillian said, "so I came over to see if you two lovebirds will leave your nest to do something fun. I mean, not too fun. I'm broke. So something local—and cheap. What do you say?"

"God. I've said this so many times, but I have to say it again. Chad's such a shit. I can't believe he was ripping off the firm, and now you're left with nothing but a bad reputation. Obviously, you can't even afford a pair of shorts that fit."

"Be quiet. I have it all. I'm doing something I really love, and I'm surrounded by people who care about me. The old house has been transformed into The Sea Sprite Inn. And even though I may be in debt for some time, I think my life, with the exception of Chad's baggage, is great."

"He's still a cheating thief," said Amy.

"Yes, he is," said Jillian.

"How about the Sea Glass Festival—ever hear of it?" Leave it to Greta to cheerfully attempt to rescue the conversation. "Tons of jewelry, lots of bad food—well bad *for* you, anyway. They have music, too. Amy and I were going. Wait. It might be this weekend, not next weekend."

Jillian's cellphone rang. "Hey, sorry. I've got to take this; my reservation line is forwarded."

"Hi, you've reached the Sea Sprite and this is Jillian. Are you ready to relax?" *Not too shabby. That sounds pretty good.*

"Hi. Umm. Yes, I guess we are. That's actually pretty

funny. You caught me off guard. I'm Mel. Your contractor, Brad, did work for some friends of mine up here in Middletown. He told us about your place."

"Great. What can I do for you, Mel?"

"I have two close friends, and every year we plan a short trip together. You know, a girls' weekend? We were wondering if you had any room for next Saturday and Sunday."

Jillian sighed but held the phone away from her mouth so her caller didn't hear her exhalation.

"Let me see. I'm pulling up the calendar. Yes, looks like I can grab an open room. Did you say there were three of you? And you want one room?" Amy grinned at Jillian pretending to consult an invisible calendar.

Mel explained they were trying to cheer up their friend Callie, who had just gone through a tough breakup.

Boy, do I know what that feels like. Like a film loop, Jillian relived the scene. She recalled how odd it was to see Chad's car at home in the afternoon. Popping in to grab her forgotten coat, she heard unfamiliar strains of music. The tune, muffled by a closed door, lured her down the hallway. The second her hand touched the doorknob, a stealthy wave of panic slapped her. The cold knob turned in her hot hand and opened the door to a nightmare.

Her husband had the firm's recent hire bent over the foot of their bed. Shiny, black high-heels peeked out between his bare feet. The gold digger had staked her claim by perforating Jillian's favorite rug with one stiletto. And it was quite obvious Chad had claimed his stake by perforating the gold digger.

"Did you get that? We'll share one room."

Jillian snapped back to the present. "Yes, OK. That should work."

Having three energetic, single girls around sounded fun. After the call, Jillian invited Amy and Greta for the weekend to make a party out of it. *Yes,* she thought, *a girls' weekend might be just the ticket.*

⚷

"See you downstairs," called Mel, as she and Rita headed down to the lobby of the Sea Sprite.

Callie pulled her old, black one-piece from the suitcase. Just as she was about to put it on, she noticed them—mocking her from their silent, little, flexible world. About a million tiny little white strands of broken, overstretched elastic poked out from every seam of her decades-old "slim-suit"—the suit which, by the way, had never touched water.

"Shit!" she yelled, dramatically throwing the suit into the corner. Then the tears started to fall. *Fat and slow, just like me,* she thought. Moments later, the slime started. God, she hated that part of a good cry.

It had been a month, but still his words echoed in her head—over and over, word for word—as if he said them yesterday. "Cal," he had started tentatively, "are you happy with me? Really happy?"

Alarms screamed in her head, and she tried to answer enthusiastically. "Of *course* I am. I love you." She inched closer to him and tried to nuzzle into his neck to get one last whiff of his scent, when he brutally cut to the chase.

"It's not working. We have different lifestyles."

Mr. Muscles, gym rat and neat freak, was finally tired of her (originally appealing) voluptuous curves, lack of interest in housekeeping, and passion for reading. Sometimes—let's be honest, most times—books took the place of chores. She tried to be a gym girl, but even with the treadmill set at only 1.5 mph, she sweated profusely, and the books she read while working out kept falling off the machine with a loud and humiliating clunk. Callie knew from reading so many romance novels, this kind of story never ended with happily ever after.

The ringing of her cellphone broke through. "Callie, it's Mel. What's taking so long?"

Callie held her breath, trying not to whimper into the phone.

"Callie, we're downstairs waiting for you. What's going on? That's it; I'm coming back up." The call clicked off.

She heard Mel taking the stairs two at a time—she really was a gym girl. Mel blew into the room and rushed the bed. She grabbed Callie's arms and forced her abruptly to her feet.

"Okay, you. It's been weeks since you've had any fun. This is our annual Rehoboth weekend, and I'm not letting you sit in here the whole time moping. We aren't going without you, so don't even try to get out of it."

"I can't go out, Mel. I don't even have a swimsuit to wear, and I just ... well ... I can't." She slumped back onto the bed. Her shiny, black hair flipped forward over her face, giving her startling blue eyes a place to hide. Mel noted that no matter how Callie landed, it always looked as though she was posed, like a curvy 1940s pinup girl waiting for the photographer.

"I call 'bullshit,' Callie. Rita is downstairs waiting. Let's go." With Mel's urging, Callie dragged herself downstairs, where Rita was intently studying the contents of the glass case in the reception area.

"What are you looking at?" asked Mel.

"Check this stuff out."

Callie gazed at the items displayed in the case. "Whoa, this is cool. I know what that one is," she said, pointing to a tiny silver purse.

"Nuh-uh. Bet you don't," teased Mel.

"Yes I do. It's an old Monopoly piece—like one of the first ones they made. My great grandpa used to make my brother and me play with him all the time. The only piece they would let me have was the purse."

"What did you say?" asked Jillian as she walked in from the kitchen.

"Callie said this little silver purse is an old Monopoly piece."

"Really?" asked Jillian. "Are you sure?"

"Yes," said Callie. "I used to play with one all the time when I was a kid."

"That's awesome. I'll do a little research on it this afternoon. I couldn't figure that one out at all."

"What are all those things, anyway?" asked Rita.

"A bit of a mystery," said Jillian, and she explained finding the "treasure" box during the renovation and her quest to find out whom it belonged to.

"Wow," said Callie. "I hope you solve it. That's a pretty cool story."

"Where are you girls headed?" asked Jillian.

"Well, we're going to do a little shopping for a bathing suit, and then we're going to the beach," said Mel. "Callie's

suit has seen better days, and she's not allowed to wear it."
Rita and Jillian laughed.

As they walked out of the Sea Sprite, Callie stopped alone for a moment to fill her lungs with the sea air and force herself to be positive. She looked up at the sign and smiled at the little sea sprite. *You're right, little sprite. I can do this,* she thought. *It's our girls' weekend, and I'm not going to ruin it.* She became a little less confident when the Rehoboth Beach shops came into view.

"Here it is," said Mel, grabbing Callie's arm and guiding her into the Pineapple Princess Swimwear Boutique.

"Pineapple Princess? Really? Now I'm a Pineapple Princess?"

"Not yet," Mel retorted. "You have to earn the title. When these ladies finish with you, you'll regret mocking it."

They stepped over the threshold and Rita took charge. She engaged the owner in a quick conversation about how Callie needed a swimsuit to show her how beautiful she was.

Callie groaned at Rita's words. They made her sound so desperate. But they only seemed to energize the owner. *Here comes the painful part,* thought Callie.

"Honey," said the owner, "you're beautiful. We just need to find the suit that feels gorgeous on you, and I think I have one. I'm guessing you're a size 14 with an F-cup bra. Is that about right?"

"Wow, I'm impressed," Callie reluctantly admitted.

The owner returned with an ordinary-looking black suit on a hanger. "Let me tell you about this one. I've had dozens of ladies report amazing results with this suit. I can't keep them in stock. Word on the street is they are pure magic. We can't prove it had anything to do with the bathing suit, but one of my customers even bought a winning Powerball ticket while wearing one."

Moments later, Callie found herself behind a green curtain, feeling like the odd little man in *The Wizard of Oz*. The black suit hung on a hook, waiting for Callie to make the first move. Callie looked in the mirror and rolled her eyes. *Okay*, she thought, *let's get this over with*. She groaned, recalling the owner's suggestion that the suit might have some sort of magical powers. Callie slipped off her flip-flops and shorts, pulled her shirt over her head, and unfastened her bra. She looked at herself in the mirror. *This is going to take some serious magic.* She reached for the suit and stepped into it. As she eased it up over her thighs and waist, it felt like it was made for her. She pulled it over her breasts, poked her arms through the straps, made a quick boob adjustment, and turned to look in the mirror.

Callie instantly knew she looked fabulous, and it showed. When she opened the dressing room door for the reveal, her waiting fans whooped and hollered their approval. Before she could blink, Callie was standing at the counter with a big-print sarong, glam sunglasses, and a wide-brimmed hat to complete the ensemble. She pulled out her card to pay, and the owner leaned over the counter toward Callie. She whispered, "I know you don't believe me, but that suit really *is* magical. Just wait and see."

⚓

Settling into the sand, Callie pulled Jennifer Weiner's book *Then Came You* out of her overstuffed bag and settled back, comfy and anonymous. Her friends bellowed to some volleyball players and then bounded away to join the game. Remembering the importance of sunscreen, she dug around in the bag, feeling for the greasy bottle. As she pulled it out, it slipped, landing right in the sand. She brushed it off the best she could before opening the cap and beginning her ministrations. Tiny grains of sand mixed with the lotion and made her application something akin to a bad exfoliation job. *So much for the magical suit,* she thought. *If it really were magic, it would've saved me from this coating of sand.* She chided herself for hoping maybe there was some scintilla of magic strengthening its elastic threads. She felt beads of sweat forming on her upper lip and between her big, awkward boobs. The droplets trailed down her chest and gathered at her belly, making her itch under the "magical" suit.

Callie slid her glam glasses down her nose and leaned back against the fluffy, red beach towels she had rolled up like pillows. She bent one shiny leg at the knee, with her foot off the towel so it could touch the life-affirming sand. She relaxed the other leg and pointed her red-tipped toes toward the water.

That was when she noticed him, sitting in the sand, alone with his camera. He was focused on the water and likely didn't notice the beautiful picture he made all on his own. The wind tousled his deep-brown hair. His shoulders were broad and tan, and he had a tattoo on his left arm she couldn't quite make out. His trunks were coral. *Coral, for God's sake.* What confidence it takes for a guy to wear coral. It was exactly the right color to set off his bronze skin.

Callie chortled to herself, thinking maybe it was *his* "magical" suit. When he stood to walk closer to the water, her eye was drawn to where his trunks began. The muscular "v" pointing from his hips led her eyes along his happy trail and made her gasp quietly. It was her favorite part of the male anatomy (almost). She didn't know what that spot was called, but she knew it made her stupid.

She spotted him again in Dolle's when the girls were buying containers of their favorite saltwater taffy. As usual, Callie didn't settle for just the taffy, so they had to wait for her caramel corn and mint sticks. Her eyes absorbed the piles of candy, eager clerks, and brightly colored displays. Then she saw him. He instantly looked away, as if she had caught him in the middle of something he was ashamed of. His camera strap and bag hung casually from his shoulder. He glanced back at Callie with sky-blue eyes that were a match to hers, smiled broadly, and waved. She swore she felt her ovaries drop onto the floor and melt into a puddle.

Callie turned around and was disappointed to see a cute little clerk wave back at him. Her cheeks went pink with embarrassment while she paid for her haul and then joined her friends on the boardwalk. She didn't mention her mystery man, but out of the corner of her eye, she watched him saunter down the boardwalk steps and head toward the water. "I think I'd like to get a little more sun," she said as casually as she could manage.

Back on the beach, she lined him up with her red toes, allowing herself to secretly watch him and fantasize. She propped open her book but kept her eyes focused above it. After several minutes of covertly stalking her stranger, she reminded herself he was probably waiting for the pretty young clerk to end her shift. On that dismal note, she lay back and directed her attention to the book. She had to admit it was a beautiful beach day; the breeze was gentle, and she tried to put herself in relaxation mode. Intoxicatingly drowsy, she allowed her eyes to close for a few moments.

She became aware the handsome stranger was looking at her. As she watched through half-closed eyes, he sat back down in the sand, facing her, and hoisted the camera to his eye. She couldn't believe it. Without being obvious, she shifted into a more appealing pose. She tried to suck in her stomach and straighten her shoulders, but it was as if she couldn't move a muscle. He was snapping pictures of her—and without asking first.

He stood up and sauntered toward her. *Oh, God.* The next moments were excruciating. Conflicting thoughts flew through her brain. "Monkey Brain," was what Mel called it. It held Callie in a death grip.

"Hey," he started tentatively. "I wanted to say hello earlier, but I needed to get down here to take a few shots of the water while the lighting was good. May I join you?"

"Of course," she replied. "I would say, 'Why don't you take a picture, it lasts longer,' but it appears you already have."

"Yes," he said, looking directly into her eyes. "Yes, I have taken some. Hope that doesn't offend you."

"I'm not easily offended, but I'm wondering why, in such a target-rich environment, you're taking pictures of me?"

He swung the camera off his shoulder and turned it on. After a few beeps and dings, he turned the camera toward her. "I'll delete all the pictures if you ask me to," he smiled, and added, "against my will."

The image on the camera screen stunned Callie. The photo showed her reclined, with the book resting on her hip. She had one arm curled over her head, and her large breasts—instead of looking awkward—sloped gracefully, creating a curve from her waist to her round hips. The line tapered into firm thighs, muscular calves, and dainty, gorgeously pedicured feet.

"You're beautiful," he said.

She felt tears building but didn't want to embarrass herself. She tried to form a sentence of thanks in her mind. He had no way to know how much it meant to hear his compliments.

Suddenly, a sharp smack on her arm roused her. "Hey there, lazybones. How long have you been asleep? You better roll over, or you're going to regret it later." Mel smirked apologetically for startling her and ran back to the volleyball game with a bottle of water and a handful of taffy. She called back over her shoulder, "Get ready—in ten minutes, we're gonna hit Thrasher's for vinegar fries and Grotto's for pizza."

Of course it was a dream.

Callie's eyes floated over the ocean of beachgoers to rest on him again. He was still there, with his camera. This time, he really was facing her. She ignored him and began packing up her bag, tossing in the sandy bottle of sunscreen. She stood up and knotted the boldly printed sarong low on her hips. She slid her feet into her flip-flops, grabbed her bag, and started walking. Her head bent, she took slow, deliberate steps toward the recently ended volleyball game. She heard rapid breathing and running footsteps right before he touched her arm.

"Excuse me," he started. "Sorry to bother you, but I can't let you get away this time without saying something. I saw you earlier when I popped into Dolle's to wave at my sister, but you were busy with your friends, and I didn't want to interrupt. I'm Michael. Look, I know this seems a little weird, but any chance you would join me for some fries?" As he turned, a Michael Connelly novel dropped out of his camera bag. He smiled, bent down, and scooped it up. "I noticed you like to read, too, and I thought maybe we could talk books?"

Callie made her decision before they reached her friends. She called out to them, "Hey guys, we're heading to Thrasher's. Meet you there."

His blue eyes brightened and his smile mirrored hers. Their discussion about literary genres over vinegar fries was intoxicating. After a few minutes, Mel and Rita had seen enough to know it was time for them to move on. Mel said to Callie, "Give me a call," and she headed toward Grotto's with Rita.

Michael and Callie continued to talk, gleefully discussing literary characters they could easily identify with. Hours later, as the sun set, they were still chatting away happily. Callie suddenly remembered something.

"Hey, what kinds of pictures do you take?" she asked, pointing to his camera.

Michael grinned, obviously pleased by her interest. "Take a look." He turned his camera over and clicked through spectacular photographs of sunrises, sunsets, ocean waves, and seashells. No shots of Callie, of course.

That was a dream, you idiot. She tried to hide her disappointment. "Gorgeous," she said, admiring the images as they flipped by.

"*You* are gorgeous. I'd love to take photographs of you sometime. You have such a natural way about you. It's as if you don't even know how beautiful you are."

Callie flushed. "Hey, I think it's time for me to head back. I really don't want to walk in the dark."

"Oh, of course." Michael hesitated. "Mind if I walk with you? I'd like to talk some more." His smile told Callie he wasn't ready to call it quits yet.

The banter between them was easy, and all too soon they stood on the verandah of the Sea Sprite. Michael reached for her hand and said, "So I'm not sure what your plans are for the rest of the weekend, but I'd really like to see you again."

"I'd like that. I'd like that a lot," said Callie.

"Can I pick you up for breakfast tomorrow morning?"

"Sounds great."

"I'll be here at nine, if that works for you."

"Sure."

Michael smiled. Then he gently brushed some sand from her shoulder and leaned in. As his lips touched hers, Callie had to wonder if maybe—just maybe—her suit really was ... *magical.*

Jillian's Journal

June 12th

Oh, my. Callie is young and thinks (like we all do at that age) there are things "wrong" with us. I hope she will see the real beauty and power within herself. Hell, I'm at fault for doing the same thing. But now? I know there's no such thing as perfection. Our beauty-at least the beauty that defines us-comes from our actions. And as for power? We have all the power (and magic) within ourselves. It's our choice whether or not we recognize it and capture the potential.

My takeaways:

One - Never forget to protect your power. We teach people how to treat us, and I will never again let someone have the ability to rent space in my head. And I will not use my emotions in place of logic.

Two - Callie, with the support of true friends, will be fine. I'm so grateful to have Amy in my life-the kind of friend you can skip seeing for months and pick up right where you left off.

Note to self - Buy some shorts that fit.

The Box: Callie told me the tiny silver purse from the box is an old Monopoly piece. I researched it and she's right! Actually found out the concept for Monopoly was created here, in Delaware, by a woman. The little purse was the eighth Monopoly piece and was introduced in 1936. It disappeared and came back several times until 1950. If it was placed here in the late thirties or early forties, that ties right in with the dates of the other treasures.

THE WEDDING CRASHERS

*J*illian walked in with her regular haul from Ginny Jo's Bakery. Thirty-five years ago, Gramps started the tradition of spending Sunday afternoons at the bakery. The routine hadn't changed in decades, with the exception of Jillian's years in Annapolis. She was happy to work with Amy and Mama Ginny. Together, they cleaned the bakery from top to bottom, making it sparkle for the week. In return for her sweat equity, Jillian got a weekly bundle of goodies for her guests. Sometimes she felt a little sad, thinking of all the years she'd missed.

Jillian carefully arranged a plate of pastries on the antique display case in the foyer. She loved this little touch of hospitality and it was free, well, almost free. *Aww ... who are you kidding,* Jillian thought, *you know who eats most of these.*

In addition to Gramps and Maegan, Amy and Mama Ginny were the only family she had, but Jillian paused a moment to consider Barb and the rest of the wonderful people she had met this year. Her family was increasing. Truth be told, the family members who surrounded her were far superior to the one she had chosen for herself.

Just like clockwork, her neighbor Barb rapped twice on the back door and walked in. "Hi, sweetcakes! Did I miss the Boston cream?"

"I always save one for you—wouldn't want to be on your bad side. Plus, you feed me a lot. I'd starve if it weren't for you."

At eighty, Barb still rode a bicycle through town, grew her own vegetables, and danced like a teenager when her favorite new-release pop songs came on. Golden oldies weren't her thing. Biting into the thick, chocolate icing, she said, "Hey, my niece called, and I referred her to you. She and her friend take a lot of trips together, but they won't stay with me. They think I'm too old for the hours they keep, so I told her to call you. Anyway, her name is Samantha, Sam for short. People say she's a lot like me, if you can believe it."

"I'd love to have them—I'm excited to meet a member of your family."

"There aren't many worth meeting," said Barb, "but this one's special. Hey, how about I give her a quick call, and we can get her scheduled?"

"Sure thing."

"All right. You take her info, but I'll foot the bill. Just don't tell her, deal?"

This was a first for Jillian. Now she had people soliciting reservations for her. She loved her peppy little neighbor. She got the feeling Gramps did, too. Maybe there was more going on between the two of them than she thought. Jillian made a mental note to invite her to the birthday party she was planning for him.

"Hey, Sammy! It's me, Aunt Babs. Listen, I'm over here at the Sea Sprite with Jillian. Yes, the one I told you about. Listen, I'm going to hand you over to her, OK? Yep, well, no time like the present." Barb held out her cell to Jillian. "Here, doll, take care of her, will you?"

"Hi. Sorry my crazy aunt put you up to this. I was going to call this afternoon," said Sam.

"No worries. Will you and your friend need two rooms or one?"

"One is fine. We'd like to come down next Friday to Sunday. Does that work?"

"That definitely works. I have a great room for you. Are there any special arrangements you need? Anything you want to do that I can help with?"

"You know, actually, there is. We choose restaurants on the internet we think would be fun to try, but we've visited Rehoboth so many times, we're running out of ideas. Do you have a recommendation that would knock our socks off?"

"Sure. Actually, there are a couple of new places you can try. When you get here we can talk about it."

"Sounds great. Thanks."

She looked forward to seeing a younger version of Barb. Jillian hoped she could muster the energy to keep up with the hours they kept.

Samantha and Kate were feeling pretty good about themselves. Sam practically pranced out of the room, excited to show Jillian her nude stilettos before they headed out for the night. Kate followed cautiously behind, doing a risk analysis of Samantha's every step from her own low-heeled shoes.

"Wow! You girls look amazing," said Jillian, closing her laptop.

"You like?" asked Samantha. She spun around with her arms in the wide frame of a dancer. She was overdressed for the beach crowd, but since they rarely had the chance to get out anymore, Sam relished the idea of kicking it up a notch. She had worn her aqua, butterfly-sleeve, one-shouldered dress with a pleated short skirt. Her blonde hair gleamed, and a chunky silver cuff bracelet signaled she was up for a challenge and she meant to win.

Conservative Kate had chosen a jersey knit in black with a longer pencil skirt that hugged her as much as she could tolerate. Kate was not a bling kind of girl, so no accessories distracted attention from her delicate neck and wrists.

"Stunners, I tell you," exclaimed Jillian.

"Oh, I almost forgot," said Kate. "I noticed the tube of lipstick in your case, and I'm a little obsessed with vintage makeup. Do you think I could ... well ... could I try it?"

"Geez, I never considered it could be useable after all these years."

Jillian shared the mystery of the box under the floor with Sam and Kate. It weighed heavily on her mind. She felt a need to push forward and solve the puzzle, but so far, there wasn't much to go on. The collection of items seemed random, but they were obviously related since the owner had them all bundled together. Jillian removed the lipstick from the case and handed it to Kate, who gingerly opened it, brought it under her nose, and sniffed.

"Well, it doesn't smell funny. I'd like to try it, if it's OK with you."

"Knock yourself out. I'm kind of excited to see what the color looks like on."

With a few quick swipes, Kate morphed into a movie star from bygone years. Ivory skin, black outfit, and red—really red—lips.

They headed for the restaurant and were relieved to find it wasn't packed. It was early, but there were already plenty of patrons in the bar.

It was split night. They had developed the tradition years ago. Each trip, they would choose a restaurant to experience. On the big night, the bill was split down the middle. Both girls would keep drinking and eating until one of them gave up because they were too nauseated or tipsy to continue. It was usually the alcohol that ended the night. This night was no different. The drinks showed up at their table faster than an attic moth finds cashmere. They did order food, but maybe not as much as they should have. Two credit cards later, they were teetering toward the boardwalk.

"What an amazing night! It's so nice out with this breeze, Kate. I don't want to go home yet. It's way too early. Let's walk down to the boardwalk and at least hang out for a while before we head back." Samantha used her whiny voice to plead for a little more action. She was used to getting her own way and knew Kate could probably be persuaded.

"OK. I'm up for it. How about we hang out on the boardwalk for a bit, and then I'll listen to you embarrass yourself at the Purple Parrot's microphone?"

Samantha nodded her head enthusiastically and started humming refrains of popular songs so she could have her list complete by the time they pulled up a barstool for karaoke.

Even though the sun had set, the Avenue was still crowded with beachgoers who seemed to have no interest in leaving: moms with dark circles under their eyes, trying unsuccessfully to shuffle gaggles of kids into Grottos for pizza, older couples clutching reading material from Browseabout Books, and middle-aged men, sitting on benches gawking at young girls in bikinis. Samantha and Kate stood out in this crowd, but as they neared the boardwalk, they noticed a steady stream of well-dressed boardwalkers drifting toward the south end.

"Come on, Kate. Let's see where they are going," said Samantha.

They turned south and walked with purpose. Although the sunbathers had left the beach, there was clearly something going on. A trellis was placed in the sand at the water's edge and was decked out with white tulle and exotic orchids. White chairs sat in straight lines on both sides. People in dressy clothes and bare feet were creating a walkway by pushing their flip-flops into the sand in straight lines.

"It's a beach wedding!" Kate exclaimed.

On tables flanking the trellis, large white candles sparkled against glass covers. Sea glass, shells, and sand filled the base of the arrangement. Both girls turned to each other and took a long inward breath.

"You're right," said Samantha. "How beautiful. Let's watch—what could it hurt?"

Kate took in the clever little touches the bride had obviously spent months planning. From the tiny twinkle lights glowing their welcome, to the conch shells hanging with satin ribbon, the atmosphere was delightful and the people looked friendly enough. Kate was reasonably certain they could pull it off without being noticed. She took Sam's arm and started walking down the stairs toward the beach. Sam smiled and graciously accepted a wedding program from a young, nervous distributor at the bottom of the boardwalk stairs who was taking his job too seriously .

In the sand, Samantha bent awkwardly to remove her shoes. Kate followed suit. Samantha—fumbling and bumbling with the clasp on her ankle straps—had all but given up before she took one good hard yank and proceeded to plunge headfirst toward the sand.

She felt her protector before she saw him. His arm shot out at the most opportune time and caught her around her waist, forcefully expelling her breath.

"Oofph!" Sam turned slowly to meet the eyes of her rescuer. "Hey, I owe you big time!"

"No problem."

"My name is Samantha; this is Kate."

He held out his suntanned hand. "Hi, I'm Mark."

As Mark took her hand and pumped it in greeting, Samantha took in his shiny, spiked, black hair, patrician nose, and blinding smile. The package was extraordinary. He looked like he had stepped out of a day spa after being plucked, buffed, waxed, and polished.

"Wow," said Kate. "I've never seen anyone move so fast. Thanks for saving Sammy here the embarrassment of pounding sand in front of all these guests. She would have been the talk of the wedding for years to come, and let's face it, who wants to be *that* story?"

They all laughed, and then Mark said, "So since I'm a groomsman for Jim—and I've never been lucky enough to meet either of you—I'm assuming you're Kelly's friends? One of her spa pals, perhaps?"

"Remarkable assumption," answered Samantha. "Obviously, I would be considered the least coordinated friend she has."

"I wouldn't say that. You should have seen her maid of

honor trying to maneuver through the sand yesterday at the rehearsal. But of course, you guys are all probably friends, so I should be careful with my loose tongue. Listen, I have to attend to some groomsman duties. Will I catch you two at the reception?"

"Of course. Wouldn't miss it," said Samantha.

The girls watched him walk away and finished removing their shoes in silence. They sidled into some empty chairs. Sam couldn't hold her excitement. She leaned in to whisper and bumped foreheads with Kate.

Rubbing her forehead, Kate sighed. "You first."

"Oh my God. I can't believe that happened. Where has he been hiding all my life? I'm telling you, when his arm caught me, I felt it. This could be the one."

"Saved from a face plant. Not only saved, but saved by your future husband who happens to be the hottest creation you've ever seen?"

Sam jabbed her elbow into Kate's arm. Kate flashed back her stink eye, perfected after years of attempting to parent her friend. Samantha leaned over and taunted, "He's mine and you're jealous. That's what's going on."

The music began quietly, drifting on the night breeze toward the crowd. The bridesmaids, arm in arm with their escorts, shuffled through the sand to take their place at the altar.

Kate took note of the thin-lipped bridesmaid clinging to Sam's Mr. Marvelous. Her eyes were focused on him and showed no signs of yielding. Mark seemed oblivious to her attentions, and instead, appeared to be scanning the crowd. When his gaze landed on the girls, he grinned and managed a slight wave in their direction. It was beyond cute. Kate watched Sam practically melt into her chair. Mark's escort looked none too happy as she followed his gaze. He whispered something to her and she shook her head, her eyes now locked on the competition.

The ceremony went off without a hitch; well technically, it ended with a hitch, and the guests all gathered to throw flower petals over the couple as they made their way back through the sand to the boardwalk. Sam and Kate grabbed their shoes and headed for the reception.

When they arrived, Mark was playing doorman. He opened the door with a gallant flourish. "Sorry, but I'm stuck here on duty for the moment. I'll look for you later, OK?"

"Of course." Samantha hung back long enough to hear the next group of friends greet Mark.

"Hi, Mark. Where's Peyton?" asked a slender redhead.

Samantha strained to hear Mark's response, but the crowd was pushing forward. So maybe Mark was attached after all, but she loved a challenge, and now it was "game on." *Peyton has no idea what she's up against,* thought Sam. *She doesn't stand a chance.*

Kate scoped out the layout for clues about the reception. Dozens of high-top tables displayed hot and cold hors d'oeuvres. She felt a wave of relief, since she hadn't figured out how they would survive a sit-down meal undiscovered. She and Kate made their way to the bar and ordered the signature wedding drink, Summer Passion.

A humorless bartender recited the ingredients of each drink he created. Samantha lost interest and wandered off, leaving Kate to suffer through the verbal checklist of measurements for their drinks.

Samantha found a seat and, glancing around, locked eyes with Mark's bridesmaid counterpart, who was making her way through the crowd in Sam's direction.

"Here we go," said Kate, as she sidled up to Sam and, noticing the approaching bridesmaid, quickly whispered, "We know Kelly from the spa. Got it?"

Sam barely had a chance to nod in acknowledgement when the satin-clad stalker reached them.

"Well, hello," she purred, a fake-friend smile plastered on her bony face. "I don't believe we've met."

"No, we haven't," replied Sam.

"Well, let me fix that. I'm Regina, a close friend of Kelly's since childhood," she claimed. "And you two?"

"Oh, we haven't known her nearly as long as you have. We met her at the spa," Sam offered.

"Which spa?" Regina asked with a sly smile.

"Those are boring details," Kate interjected. She placed her hand gently on Regina's shoulder and said, "I just want to say you and Mark make a fabulous couple."

Regina flushed. "Oh wow, umm, we aren't actually a couple. I just met him recently, but that's nice of you to say."

"You're so lucky!" Kate continued, "All the girls here want to trade places with you, right Sam?"

"Yep, for sure," said Samantha, "but they've all given up. He obviously only has eyes for you."

"Well, it was nice meeting you. I'm sure we'll bump into each other again before the night is out." She turned and flitted away with a Cinderella smile pasted to her lips.

"Dang," sighed Sam. "You're good. I mean, really good. I never would've thought that up."

"People like that are easy reads. You feed her what she wants to hear, and she thinks you're on her side. I feel sorry for Mark, though. We'll definitely need to rescue him from her clutches. Now that I've encouraged her, she'll be stuck to his behind like bumper-to-bumper beach traffic on Route 1."

About the time the guests reached a happy balance between food and drink, the music started. Sam and Kate were enjoying both the people-watching and the Summer Passions. Samantha was hoping for an opportunity to talk with Mark alone, but Regina seemed to have her talons firmly embedded into his forearm. The minute Regina was pulled onto the dance floor by a group of bridesmaids, Sam saw Mark make a mad dash for the bar. Then he made his way toward their table, carrying an orange drink complete with its own umbrella.

"Whew. Regina is sure a talker. Thought I'd never get away from her. Can I get you ladies anything?"

"Depends." Sam glibly mocked Kate with her glance and asked, "Are your rescue reflexes still on point? Because I could really use a whirl around the dance floor. Are you up for it?"

"Well ... I ... uh ...," stammered Mark.

Samantha pushed her drink into one of Kate's hands and grasped Mark's arm, leading him to the dance floor. "Oh, come on; it's no big deal."

Mark threw a beseeching glance toward Kate, silently pleading for a rescue, but she knew better than to try to save him from Sam. Instead, she shrugged an implied apology for her friend's enthusiasm.

They eased onto the crowded dance floor. Sam was having so much fun, she neither felt, nor saw, the daggers being thrown into her back by Regina. She slipped her hand around the back of Mark's neck and gently trailed her fingernails on his exposed skin. He responded by quickly twirling her away from him and ending in a dramatic dip. Like a bad version of musical chairs, when the orchestra stopped playing, they were directly in front of Regina. Deep in the dip, neither of them noticed her vicious foot snake out and wrap around Sam's weight-bearing leg.

It happened so fast, balancing was out of the question. Sam tumbled to the floor, and this time, Mark followed her lead. Samantha's elbow caught one of the high-top tables, and Mark's hip took down the second. They ended up in a discombobulated heap amidst finger foods, floating orchids, and drink umbrellas.

"Are you—"started Mark.

"Oh my God. I'm so embarrassed," said Sam, breaking into a laugh.

They looked at each other, and then laughter turned into full-out chortling, with a couple of good-measured snorts thrown in.

Kate rushed over. "Why in the hell would she do that? You could have been hurt."

"Do what?" asked Mark.

"That bridesmaid—Regina. She tripped you on purpose. I saw her. Unbelievable!"

Mark turned to Samantha to help her up. Sam, spurred on by the Summer Passions, took advantage of the moment and leaned in to try for a kiss. Instead of meeting her halfway, Mark backed out of kissing range and politely extended his hand to help Samantha to her feet. Not the reaction she had hoped for. She had expected a passionate kiss while a choir of angels serenaded them, but she got nothing. Zip. Nada. Zilch. Zero. Even worse, a fuming Regina was leading the bride straight to them.

"Uh oh," said Kate.

Kelly approached Mark and, gesturing toward Kate and Sam, asked, "Are these two friends of yours?" Regina's face was a smug sneer.

Kate beat him to a response. "Do you realize your bridesmaid intentionally tripped them? They could have been hurt. Why don't you ask her what the hell she was thinking?"

Trying to de-escalate the rising drama, Mark answered Kelly. "Yes, actually, they are friends of mine. I told Jim that Peyton might not make it tonight, and he didn't think you'd mind if I invited a couple of other people instead."

They were interrupted by a strong voice over the microphone announcing the bouquet toss. The bride— looking somewhat skeptical—trotted off to perform for her guests.

Just then, Mark's face lit up with a huge grin. Kate followed his gaze.

A spectacularly good-looking man was coming their way at a rapid clip. "There you are! What happened? Jim told me you fell! Are you ok? Sorry I'm so late. Forgive me?" Kate pulled the dumbfounded Samantha out of their way.

"Sam, Kate, Regina," said Mark. "This is Peyton, my date."

"Peyton?" repeated Sam with an incredulous whisper.

Mark assessed the stunned look on the faces of the women surrounding him. It wasn't the first time this had happened. "Uh oh, I assumed Kelly would've told you about Peyton. Sorry."

With a venomous hiss, Regina stormed off in a cloud of black karma and hideous satin.

Sam's pride was a little bruised, but it wouldn't last long; it never did. With a sheepish grin, she responded the only way she could.

"Anyone up for some more Summer Passion?" she asked with a wink.

Jillian's Journal

August 2nd

Energy. Opposites. Youth. Enthusiasm. Sam and Kate were wonderful girls. I was worried I wouldn't be able to keep up with them, but a funny thing happened. Being around the energy actually infused me with more. It makes so much sense. People want to be around Barb because of her positivity. It's a win/win because she is invigorated by them. I used to hide from people who are overloaded with energy, but now I welcome them—at least in limited doses.

My takeaways:

One – Relationships are best between people who balance, like Kate and Sam. Both add something to the other's life. Good characteristics complement what the other may need more of. Negative traits may exist, but they don't deplete the other. Most people have habits that frustrate me. If they don't subtract from my quality of life, those annoying habits aren't of consequence. The good in friends will supplement my shortcomings, and my good will do the same for them.

Two – Live every day.

Watching Kate try the lipstick, I clearly pictured it years ago, gliding across a young girl's lips, wanting to tempt a lover. I read that during the war, Winston Churchill claimed lipstick was a morale booster. In 1941, the US Marine Corps Women's Reserves asked Elizabeth Arden to create "Victory Red" to match their uniforms. I'm going to ask Gramps about it. I bet he has plenty of stories to tell.

THE DRIFTERS

*L*ife can get so complicated. Jillian remembered the call from Marjorie. She had sounded so excited about the prospect of taking her husband and his assistant to the beach for a week of rejuvenating sunshine.

"Hello? Hello? Oh, Lord, is it ringing? Amanda? Your phone isn't as loud as mine." The woman was obviously experiencing some difficulty. Jillian waited patiently.

"Hello?" she tried again.

"Hello, you've reached The Sea Sprite Inn, this is Jillian." *Better stick with simple this time,* she thought.

"Oh, my. Yes, there you are. I can hear you now. Oh, dear, I'm sorry. I'm Marjorie. I'm calling to make a reservation for my husband, our assistant, Amanda, and me."

Her voice sounded so cheerful and kind, Jillian was immediately curious about her.

"Great. What dates did you have in mind?"

"I'm thinking August, but not during a holiday week. We don't want to be packed in like sardines. Just want to come down to relax, take in some sun together, and walk the beach at sunset. Is the Sea Sprite close to the boardwalk?"

"August is a great month here, and I do have two rooms open the third week. We're two blocks off the beach. The sunsets are wonderful, and you'll be in great company—

the drifters wait until the youngsters leave before they take their turn on the beach."

"The drifters? You mean homeless people?"

"Oh, no, I'm sorry. Drifters is what I call people who walk the beach at sunset. I'm included in the group. Cranberry Park is close and so is Lake Gerar. It's a great area; I think you would love it here."

"Oh, it sounds lovely. I need to prepare you a bit for our visit. Can you hold one second so I can get to the other room?"

Jillian heard Marjorie's footsteps, and then what sounded like a door closing and the scrape of a wooden chair being pulled across the floor.

"I'm back. Are you still there?"

"I'm still here."

"Well, dear, I think I need to let you know that my husband has dementia. Amanda is wonderful with him, and I do the best I can, but sometimes it can be a bit challenging. Do you think it will be a problem?"

"Since you have a caregiver with you, I doubt there would be anything we couldn't handle. How far has your husband's dementia progressed? Do you have any safety concerns for him?"

"He can still feed himself, dress, shower, walk, and use the restroom on his own. He repeats stories and questions. It can be a bit overwhelming. This isn't the way we thought our life would turn out, but here we are."

Jillian hung up, tears in her eyes. *I can't imagine.* She often longed for the future she had planned for and then lost when Chad signed their divorce papers, but Marjorie's loss seemed far greater. To watch your soulmate slowly slip away. . . .

The silver Buick bumped over the curb and moved down the length of the driveway, its tires crunching stones under each revolution. Marjorie expected the Sea Sprite to be on the street, but the driveway led between two curbside properties. As she passed those homes, a solid screen of pines came into view.

For some people, missing curb frontage would have been a negative, but Marjorie thought it a perfect setting. As the car glided through the opening in the trees, Marjorie got her first glance of The Sea Sprite Inn and was instantly charmed.

She stopped the car and, with the flick of a switch, opened the passenger window so she could absorb the details. Bright, glossy, periwinkle gingerbread trim framed the cheery white exterior, and shutters sporting starfish cutouts surrounded each window. Pink and purple flowering vines climbed the pillars, reaching the bottom of the second-floor balcony, which was enclosed by white panels with more starfish cutouts. Pots overflowing with flowers lined the steps and walkway. Marjorie would never have thought to use all those colors together, but they drew her in, and she could feel her pensive mood disappearing. A small smile climbed the corners of her mouth, and by the time she had put the car back into drive, it had spread into a grin. She pulled the car into a visitor spot in the side yard under a striped canopy.

Grabbing her weekend bag from the trunk, she stepped onto the path leading to the front door. Pausing to smooth her gray, tailored jacket, she tugged at her jeans, smoothing the wrinkles acquired during the drive, and adjusted her necklace. A rectangle of gray stone nestled among the patterned web of lines across décolletage that tattled her age to anyone who was interested. Running her hand through her hair for a final touch, she made her way to the front door, glancing at the sign over the entranceway. *I could use a sprinkling of the magic dust you've got there, sea sprite.*

Before she could knock, the door swung open and a woman emerged. Marjorie took in the woman's denim shorts, crocs, and whimsical batik tunic. She noticed a smudge of blue paint across her cheek. *An artist, perhaps?*

"Oh, hi," said the woman. "I'm Jillian. You must be Marjorie. Here, let me help you with that." She reached for the bag and, wrapping her free hand around Marjorie's shoulder, gave her new guest a welcoming half-hug.

"Yes. Thanks for the help," said Marjorie, following Jillian into the inn. "I'm so sorry about having to cancel the reservations for my husband and Amanda. Patrick's been so confused lately." Marjorie's voice broke. "I caught him downstairs at one in the morning, trying to start the electric stove with a lighter. It wouldn't have been safe."

"You did the right thing. It must have been difficult for you to come here on your own, but I'm glad you did. Hopefully, you'll find some new energy while you're here. Don't worry another second about the reservations. It happens all the time."

"Call me Marge; everyone does." Her eyes made a quick sweep of the foyer. "The Sea Sprite is beautiful. I couldn't have asked for anything better." As she spoke the words, Marge sighed deeply, realizing how thankful she was for this escape, even if it was brief. Calm enveloped her as Jillian's words soaked in. *It's true,* she thought. *My only responsibility this weekend is to re-energize.*

"Tell you what. How about we start your visit with a little tour? Afterward, you can explore on your own. I'll just put the kettle on."

While Jillian filled the teapot, Marjorie noticed a large

sculpture made from driftwood. It served as a room divider and stood at least six feet tall. So many colors, shapes, and sizes, but together they made quite a statement.

"Where did you get this?" she asked.

"Would you believe I made it?"

"Stunning. I've never seen anything like it."

"I love to use walks on the beach for introspection. Somehow I started picking up driftwood. Even though it's cast off and weathered, I think it has even more value and beauty. When my collection grew to over a hundred pieces, I decided to create something I could use. Like me, it's wrinkled, but still useful."

Marjorie smiled knowingly. "My husband spent forty years as the founder of his own company wearing suits, ties, and wingtips. Now he's a loveable, breakfast aficionado who wears sweat suits and fleece-lined slippers. His life revolves around cable television, protein supplements, and incontinence supplies."

As she spoke, Marjorie wondered. *What am I doing? This is too personal—why am I telling her this?* But the intrusive thoughts were fleeting. She realized how much she missed having someone to share her worries and frustrations with.

"Before this year," she continued, "the toughest decisions I had to make were selecting dinner menus and choosing charity functions. I stayed home, played tennis, and shopped with my friends. Now my days are scheduled in fifteen-minute increments. Everything is a strict routine. I don't even have time to take a bath, let alone figure out a path forward."

"Wow." Jillian's voice was barely a whisper. "That sounds overwhelming."

"It is. You know, years ago, we both said if either of us were ever incapacitated, the other would choose a full-time care facility to take over. We wanted our healthy partner to live—really live —and find their own happiness. But it's not easy." She took a sip of tea and dabbed her mouth with a napkin. "I signed him into a facility this weekend to test it out. I need him to be someplace he's safe, but the guilt is tough."

"Marge, I can't begin to imagine how hard it must be to go through that with your husband. My grandfather had a stroke recently, and I moved from Annapolis to help. He's in rehab at a nursing home, so I understand a little of what you're going through. You're right; the guilt is horrible."

"It sure is. At first you wake up each day and do what needs doing. Then one day you notice the pain, and like a nagging toothache, it comes and goes. Finally, the pain becomes the only thing you feel and you learn to welcome it—it means you're alive."

"Exactly. I just keep pushing forward. I'm hoping to be able to bring him back here soon. I'm not sure how much time we have left, but whatever is left, I want to spend it with him."

Marjorie paused to sip the reassuring chamomile. Leaning in, she gently rested her cup on its matching saucer. "Friday was our forty-third anniversary and—" Marjorie paused to wipe a tear with a discreet swipe of her hand, "he doesn't even know my name."

⚷

The next morning, the soft cooing of the resident mourning doves jostled Marjorie awake. She lay quietly, absorbing the fact that she was actually at the beach alone. Leaves danced on the breeze in front of her window, throwing shadows against the ceiling. A splash of blue in the gray sky hinted the day might turn into perfection. She showered, dressed, and followed the scent of freshly ground coffee beans to the lobby. The steaming percolator welcomed her with a gurgle. After pouring her first cup of coffee on top of a generous helping of fresh cream, Marge noticed an antique display case. As she walked toward it, she heard Jillian softly clear her throat.

"Good morning. I see you found my little display." Jillian explained she had discovered the items in a box during renovation. "It's been tough to figure out what each trinket is and what the connection might be. I'm hoping one day it will all come together and the mystery will be solved."

Marjorie headed for the beach, realizing her day was unstructured for the first time in ages. It was exhilarating to have time to herself. *Rejuvenation.* She wanted to remind herself of who she was when life was young and carefree. She remembered how she used to enjoy long walks as a young girl. The thoughts were random, but they took her back to happier days. As she walked, she realized she was enjoying the anonymity. *Sometimes you want to go where no one knows your name.*

She hesitated, then broke into an awkward skip, ignoring the amused looks of some people she passed on Olive Avenue. Although her skip resolved into a brisk walk by the time she reached the boardwalk, the items in her beach bag had begun to spill out of its open top. Pausing, she readjusted the towel, umbrella, newspaper, notebook, and bottle of sunscreen.

It was still early, and the beach was just waking. Sand massaged the soles of her feet with a tickle, pressing up into her arches. It carried morning coolness through her toes.

The light breeze from the shore smelled strongly of sausage, while fluffy egg-white clouds dotted the gray-blue sky.

Having chosen her spot, she carefully unknotted the tails of the white linen shirt she had tied around her waist. Her hair blew freely, spreading like a silver crown in the breeze. She lowered herself onto her beach blanket and scooped out several concave divots to cradle her behind.

The only goal this morning was to write her thoughts down as they came to her. Stretching, she grabbed The Sea Sprite Inn notebook and sat quietly, pen poised above the paper. Nothing came to her. Putting the notebook down, she slowly rose to her feet and began walking. She wanted to feel, not think.

Strolling along the waterline, she saw several other people walking toward her. *What was it Jillian had called them? Ahh, yes—drifters.* They walked the shore aimlessly, just as she had described, each of them—each of *us*, she corrected herself—searching for something. The obvious question had her stumped. *What are you searching for, Marjorie?* It was a great question, but she had no idea what the answer was.

She walked on the water-packed sand, alternating her gaze between the waves and the beach. The sun hadn't risen high enough to really warm the air. Several of the drifters wore windbreakers and baseball caps. The wind picked up, stirring goose bumps on her forearms and thighs. A blanket of clouds moved over the sun, casting a dark-gray shadow on the beach. A shiver ran through her, but she welcomed it, thankful she had the ability to notice.

She saw a group of drifters head for the stairs to the boardwalk and noticed families were arriving with crowded strollers and overloaded beach totes. A few early morning runners were making mental checkmarks before turning to their next "to do" on the list.

As she walked, Marjorie had asked herself at least a dozen times, "What are you searching for, Marjorie?" She turned around to head back toward her blanket. Another drifter passed. The woman's eyes were blank and her face expressionless. Not a glimpse of joy.

I know that look. For years, Marjorie had watched her husband's life slowly slip away—not because of the dementia, but because he had stopped living. The more she entertained this thought, the more she realized many of her friends had reached the same point. They weren't growing; they had no interest in learning new things or the desire to feel alive again. They had reached a plateau and stayed there.

As the dark clouds shifted, sunshine filled the sky. Tilting her face to the warmth, Marjorie felt a shift in her soul. She didn't want her life stolen from her. There was much for her to give and even more to learn. She needed to be vital. *Life is a cycle,* she thought, noting the beach had changed again. The drifters were replaced by families: babies held at the water's edge, being dipped into the surf with waterlogged diapers, and mothers—unwilling to let a painful sunburn damage the fun—diligently plastering their tots with white lotion. The smell of baby powder and sunscreen, not breakfast sausage, now filled the air.

Marjorie reached her blanket and settled into her custom sand divots. She was thinking now, and all of her senses were sharpened. Pen in hand, words began to fill the page.

Her train of thought was interrupted by a low beep. The light, but persistent, tone niggled into her head and made her glance up from her notebook. A man in a button-down shirt, elasticized shorts, and brown water sandals with black socks waved a metal detector back and forth over the sand as he walked along the beach. A giggle escaped Marjorie's mouth. *What a picture he paints,* she thought, and then felt guilty. *Could I be more judgmental?*

The man held his head at an awkward angle, obscuring his face from Marjorie's view. His shirt sported a pocket with a notebook and pens, and he wore a bulging black pack on his back. *He must take this stuff pretty seriously.* A mop of grayish-brown curls touched the top of his collar and sprang up and down with each sweep. Marjorie couldn't help but chuckle again. She was still smiling when she heard the frequency and volume of the detector increase dramatically. The man circled the area, and when the tone went to a flat singular alarm, he jumped straight up.

"Gotcha!" He looked in her direction. "Did you hear that? Come on over and give me a hand. This is gonna be somethin'—somethin' big."

Marjorie looked around to see who he was speaking to. When she didn't see anyone in close enough range, she looked back at him.

"Come on, then."

She raised her eyebrows and pointed to herself, mouthing "Me?"

He answered with an excited nod. She shook her head back and forth to indicate no, but he repeated, with emphasis, "Come *on*, give me a *hand.*"

Marjorie hesitated but then remembered she was trying to bring a little levity and life back into her game. She left her solitude and covered the thirty feet quickly, her decision based solely on his enthusiasm.

"There you go." He reached around and took off his backpack—letting it slide to the beach—and then unzipped it and looked inside. He offered her a perforated metal scoop and took the small shovel for himself.

"OK," he started. "Here's what you're gonna do. You're gonna scoop away as much sand as you can from this circle." Flushed with excitement, he indicated an area by drawing a jagged circle about eighteen inches in diameter with his shovel. Marjorie was surprised to see he was actually not bad looking—sort of a chubby, geeky Harrison Ford with curly hair.

"OK, uhh," he hesitated. "What's your name anyway?" His eyes rested on hers and he waited.

"My name is Marjorie, but most people call me Marge."

"OK, Marge," he said with a grin, "you ready for a treasure hunt?"

She returned his grin and nodded her head.

"Well, get to it, then."

She stuck her scoop in the center, filled it with sand, carefully carried it outside the border of the designated dig circle, and dumped it behind her.

"I'm John. Just John," he said. "Nice to meet you."

"Do you always enlist the help of strangers for your treasure hunts, Just John?"

He laughed. "Not always, but you were watching me pretty closely, and you looked like one of those kids who wants to join the game but waits for an invitation."

Both of them cleared sand away until they reached the wet layer. John eased up from his knees to a standing position. He put one sandaled foot on the top of the mini-shovel, and pushed it deep into the wet sand. He took the first shovelful and dumped it next to him.

"All right, Marge, dig down into the sand. When your scoop's full, lift it and give it a few shakes like you're sifting flour. Got it?"

"Wait, you want *me* to sift it? Why don't *you* sift it?"

"Don't be silly, girl. Give it a try."

"Fine," she retorted, and dug the scoop into the sandy muck. The wet sand was heavier and took some energetic shaking to get it through the holes in the sifter. She heard a slight clink after the last shake and peered into it. "I think there's something here."

"There better be," answered John, "or I paid way too much money for this Minelab E-Trac." He laughed. "Actually, I really did pay too much money for it, but that's another story."

Marjorie cleared the last bits of sand away. "It's a ring," she exclaimed, and held it up for John to examine.

"Whoa, girl. You got yourself a nice one."

"Is it real?"

"Real? Sister, you got yourself a genuine Dollar Store ring on your first dig. Not real, but real pretty." He smirked. "Put it on and see if it fits."

Marjorie slid the ring on her middle finger. The large oval pink stone was flanked by two smaller round stones of the same color. It was actually kind of pretty.

"Well, I'll be darned. It's a fit."

Marjorie took the ring from her finger and held it out to John. "Wow, good for you. That really was more fun than I thought it would be. Thanks for inviting me to help."

John pushed her hands back and closed her fingers over the ring. "Oh no, I'm not taking your treasure. I have a rule: whoever scoops it, keeps it. Besides, I can't think of a nicer lady to give it to. Just make sure your husband doesn't get mad at me. I see you're sporting a real nice set of wedding rings."

"My husband probably won't notice," she explained. "He has dementia. I'm just resting up here for a couple of days before I head back home."

"Oh, I'm real sorry to hear it. Sounds tough."

"Thanks. It is tough. Surely you have someone who would like this ring?"

"Nope. No wife, no mother, no. . . ." He paused. "No lady to give it to. So there you have it. Your new ring—must be your lucky day."

Marjorie was surprised he wanted her to keep it, but since she had spent the better part of the morning deciding she needed to get out of her comfort zone a bit, she graciously accepted the ring as a silly gift.

"Hey, can I ask you a favor?" He didn't wait for an answer before continuing. "If I set my stuff down next to your blanket there, could you keep an eye on it for, say, an hour?"

Caught off guard, Marjorie answered hesitantly, "I suppose so. Is this payment for the ring?"

"No," he said with a laugh. "I need to run an errand, and I hate having to lug all this stuff with me. If I'm not back by twelve thirty, you can leave it all here and go. Deal?"

"OK, deal. I'll babysit till twelve thirty."

What a strange morning. Smiling at the unexpected turn her day had taken, Marjorie picked up her notebook to begin another entry. She looked around her now, and although only an hour or so had passed, the beach had gone through yet another transition, definitely worthy of recording. She wrote until she couldn't ignore her hunger pangs anymore and reached for the bag of pretzels. Crunching away, she observed her surroundings. She was fascinated by the ebb and flow of the people and the water and wanted to see if she could describe it. Finished with her first page, she set the pen down and stood, and as she did, she heard a voice call out from behind.

"Hey, Marge! Don't leave—I'm back."

Marge turned and grinned in spite of herself. There he was, trudging through the sand in his Velcro-strapped sandals and black socks, balancing a Nicola's bag and drinks.

"Perfect timing."

He handed her the containers. "I thought it was the least I could do since you watched my stuff for me."

Marjorie noticed him looking at her notebook. Wanting to keep her observations private, she gently closed it and placed it into the beach tote.

"I was happy to. After all, you did give me a present, right? How could I say no?"

"You've got a point," John answered, and opened the Nicola's bag to reveal two Nic-o-boli overstuffed sandwiches. "So you can split the tab with me if you're feeling guilty, but I like buying pretty ladies lunch—especially if they let me eat with them."

"Charmer," Marge answered. "Of course you can eat with me."

She groaned with pleasure as her teeth crunched through the warm, crispy bread and sank into the seasoned beef and cheese. The only sounds either of them made were ohhhs, mmmms, and ahhs until each of them came up for air at the halfway mark.

"Wow," Marge exclaimed. "That hit the spot. Thanks."

"You're welcome. Glad you like them. They're one of my favorites."

"So I'm curious. You said earlier you didn't have a lady in your life to give the ring to. Is that intentional?"

As she watched, John's smile evaporated. He crossed his arms and looked away. When he turned back to face her, his eyes reflected an intimate pain. She knew the look and had likely worn the same expression often over the years.

"Tell you what. I'd really rather not talk about it. I will say I have no companionship other than my sister, who is in a wheelchair and unable to speak. I visit her a lot, but it gets lonely sometimes."

"I'm sorry."

"It's OK. I just don't really want to talk about it."

"I understand. I feel the same way about my husband's illness. I don't really want to talk about that, either." She smiled and changed topics.

For the next few hours, their conversation jumped across more subjects than she would have believed. Every so often, Marge took note of the changes on the beach. The new crowd shuffling in each time was different from the last. She wanted to remember so she could continue writing later, when she was alone.

"So tell me, why do you hang out on the beach with your metal detector?"

At this, John's face instantly lifted. "Did you know metal detectors have been used since 1881? Heck, the first documented use was by Alexander Graham Bell, who was trying to locate the bullet in President James Garfield's chest."

"I had no idea."

"And a guy in California found a piece of gold they called the Mojave Nugget. It's worth thousands. People have found treasure worth over a million and a half bucks with these things. Now I'm not saying I think I'm gonna get rich here, but it sure brings a smile to my face when I find something shiny."

"Wow," said Marge. "Can you imagine finding a haul like that? Not quite on that level, but the lady who owns the Sea Sprite told me about a great place I can look for driftwood. If it's as secret as she said it was, maybe it would be a great place to use your metal detector. You're welcome to check it out with me tomorrow. I planned on going after everyone leaves the beach."

"Hmm. The locals know all the great spots. All right, I'm game, as long as you let me pick the place to eat. What do you say, you game?" he smiled broadly and waited for her answer.

Marjorie hesitated for only a moment before answering. "Well, as long as we aren't talking about a date, I'll say yes."

"All righty. And it's not a date—I'd never ask a married woman on a date. This is a treasure search. Let's meet at the Blue Moon at 6:30. It's pretty fancy, but I don't know how much more fried food from the boardwalk I can take."

Marjorie stood, and with a smile, she began packing her beach tote. "OK, just so we're clear, I'm paying for my own meal."

⚷

On her way back to the Sea Sprite, Marjorie called Sunrise Senior Living to check on her husband. She was relieved—and a bit surprised—by the positive report. He was eating well and participating in the activities. She could relax. When Marjorie opened the back door of the Sea Sprite, Jillian was busy preparing dinner in the kitchen.

"So how was your day?"

Marjorie shared the story of her treasure hunt and showed off the ring. "If you looked on the internet for pictures of a metal-detecting old guy on the beach, I have no doubt John's picture would pop up. It's the 'Nerdy Grandpa' look. You know what I mean, don't you? Shorts, black socks, brown sandals, and spindly legs—it made quite a picture."

The two ladies tittered, and within seconds, couldn't contain their laughter. Jillian set the knife down, turned on the water, and splashed her face with moist hands, trying to stop laughing long enough to catch a breath. It hadn't been exceptionally hilarious, but it seemed both of them were already on the edge of giddiness and couldn't (or wouldn't) let go of the joke. Each time she looked at Marjorie, a new round of laughter would begin. Howling, Jillian spurted out, "Good thing for panty liners." Both women roared with a renewed vigor. After several sessions of gasping, they finally regained some composure.

"Well," started Jillian, "at least he gave you a cute ring. There must be something you like about him other than his wardrobe choices, right?"

"You know, he seems like such a nice guy and there was no pressure. I feel comfortable with him. Actually, we are going to meet up again tomorrow for a bite to eat and then head over to the driftwood area you told me about."

"For your sake, I hope his dinner wardrobe doesn't involve sandals and socks."

Marjorie headed to bed for an early turn-in, but it didn't exactly work out. She felt exhausted when she climbed into bed, but found herself thrashing instead of sleeping. After ending up with her legs tangled in the sheets and her feet hanging over the edge of the bed, she surrendered. She grabbed her novel and spent the next three hours reading.

When Marjorie woke in the morning, the novel was on the bed, but the words on the open page weren't familiar. She had stopped comprehending long before her eyes had finally closed the night before. This morning, she planned to borrow Jillian's bicycle and ride around Rehoboth. She hadn't ventured far from this little corner of the beach, and she was eager to see more of the town.

The wheels spun slowly, and her casual pedaling generated enough breeze to keep her hair dancing. Bikes were allowed on the boardwalk until ten, so there was plenty of time to traverse its length. She rode to Queen Street and turned up King Charles Avenue. After making a wiggle onto 1st Street, she headed back to the boardwalk and down Wilmington Avenue. But when she spotted Cafe Papillon, her empty stomach complained. The line was long, but it would be worth the wait. After ordering coffee, along with a salmon, sour cream, and chives crepe, she gave in and added a banana and Nutella crepe, just to make sure she had enough energy for the ride back.

Sitting at an outside table, Marjorie relaxed. *I miss Patrick, but I really needed this.* She promised herself she would make this an annual event—no matter what happened.

Marjorie washed down the last bite of crepe with a final sip of coffee, stood, and stretched. *What a great town this is.* She got back on the bicycle and rode by a line of shops until a colorful top called out to her from its hanger on a rack in front. She parked the bike and went inside to try it on. It would be ideal for her dinner with John. *Silly,* she thought. *This isn't a date—you're being ridiculous.*

The rest of the morning she cruised side streets, slowing to look at the spectacular homes. As early afternoon approached, she wound her way back to the Sea Sprite and returned the bicycle, balancing it against the wall for support. *What a wonderful day this is turning out to be.*

⚷

A few hours later, Marjorie was showered, shampooed, perfectly coiffed, and dressed in a beachy outfit that included her new top. She came down the stairs and heard a familiar song playing in the foyer.

"Oh, my," Marjorie said. "I just realized something." She moved to the display cabinet. "Jillian, do you know what these are?" Marjorie asked, pointing to the ragged, torn tickets.

"They look like movie tickets, but I have no idea how old they are, or even what the movie was."

Marjorie chuckled. "Look at the top left corner. I think the 'C' might stand for *Casablanca*. I haven't thought of that movie for a few years, but I heard the theme song on your radio. It was our favorite movie. We watched it snuggled up in theatres, cuddling in front of the TV, parked in front of a VCR, and even viewed it on DVD."

"*Casablanca*. Of course. That makes sense. I wonder what year it came out," said Jillian.

"Oh, that's easy, 1943. I know because my mother always joked the reason I was here was because of that movie, and I was born in '44. My husband heard the story and from then on, it was always the same. I'd say, 'Of all the gin joints, in all the towns, in all the world, I had to walk into yours.' Then he'd answer, 'Here's looking at you, kid.' We always finished with, 'Kiss me as if it were the last time.' " *When was the last time he kissed me? I hadn't even realized it was the last time. Was it really the last time?*

The room was silent for a moment.

"Well, I'll bet these tickets hold a special place in the heart of whoever owned them," said Marjorie. "I sure hope you solve the mystery."

"Me, too, Marjorie. Me, too." With a wave and a "good luck" from Jillian, Marjorie made her way to dinner.

John was waiting for her in front of the restaurant dressed in a linen jacket with an open-collar blue shirt and dark pressed jeans. Glancing at him, she almost laughed out loud when she noticed he was still wearing the same sandals, but she was grateful he was also wearing the same smile.

"Hey now. This is exactly what I've been looking forward to all day." John turned and opened the door for her. He ordered a bottle of the house white on the way to the table. They were seated—menus in front of them—and the conversation already had taken off.

"So where are you taking me for treasure hunting?" asked John. Their wine arrived, and he edged his large frame toward her to allow the server extra room.

"It's a little bit up the beach. I'm not sure how much you'll find there this late, but it's nice out, and Jillian said the dunes will be pretty."

"Sounds great. So I noticed you writing yesterday. What are you writing about?"

"I was writing about the beach and how it changes in cycles, like life in general. I guess I'm doing a little soul-searching in addition to driftwood hunting."

"We've all done that at one point or another. I used to, but I don't search for anything but beach treasures anymore.

I'm happy with what I have, and I think if life is meant to be different, it'll find me."

During dinner, Marjorie told John about Patrick and his struggles with dementia. John casually reached across the table, patting her hand in support while she spoke. After admitting her heartbreak at not being recognized anymore, she confided she was ready for a new start to her life. "I came here to re-energize, but I guess what I really needed to do was regain my passion for living."

"You seem like a strong woman. I feel lucky to have met you."

"Well, enough about me. I'd really like to know your story."

John paused, as if deciding what to say. "I think what matters is the here and now. How I got here isn't really important; I'm just thankful to be here." Marjorie smiled. She wouldn't press for details.

"Speaking of which—" John stood and, with a flourish, waved his arms high in the air and motioned for the check.

The sun had dipped under the horizon, and the beach was tucked in for the night. Moonlight threw glitter sparkles across the water and magically danced on the top of each wave. The day's heat was gone, but Marge was comforted by the solid warmth of John next to her. The sound of the sea running toward the beach was cleansing after the din of the packed restaurant. They were close to the tide, and a bit of sea spray sprinkled Marjorie's lips. She ran her tongue over the saltiness.

John caught the move. "Thirsty?" he asked. "I can run back and grab you a margarita."

She laughed. "I think not."

John stopped walking and faced the ocean. Without looking directly at her, he began to speak softly.

"Thirty-two years ago. It was thirty-two years ago when my wife left. She took my two-year-old daughter with her, and I haven't seen either of them since. I've looked. God knows, I've looked. I've spent hundreds of hours and thousands of dollars trying to find them. I can't seem to give up—it's what keeps me awake at night."

"I'm so sorry," Marjorie said. "That must be agonizing."

"In those days, I worked long hours, so maybe she felt lonely. Oh hell, she must have *been* lonely. I was never around. She met someone and had an affair. When I found out about it, I swore to her I would be a better husband, a better father." John's eyes remained focused on the water. "She said we could try and I believed her. But the next day when I came home early with flowers, they were gone. I told you earlier I wasn't searching for anything, but that's a lie. I am searching. I'm always searching."

Marjorie didn't say a word, but she couldn't help thinking, *and here I am, letting life roll by without searching enough.* She stood next to him, watching the water. When the moment had passed, they began to walk again. The moon lit the tops of the grasses, and shadows passed across the dunes. Each of them carried their shoes, feeling the land release the heat of the day under their toes as they entered the dune line.

"Owww!" John's body jerked. He grabbed her, attempting to balance, but then tumbled into the sand.

Margaret knelt next to him. "What happened?"

"My toe. I stubbed it. Dang, that hurts like a ... that *hurts.*"

Marjorie, trying to repress a smile, looked where they had just been walking. She spotted what he had hit. She shimmied back to John's side to present it.

"I found it."

"Found what?"

"Your treasure." She held it in front of him so he could see it. "You tripped on a piece of driftwood."

John sat up with his elbows supporting him in the sand, and his face cracked a huge grin. "Well, I'll be darned."

Marjorie triumphantly plopped down and set the wood next to her in the sand. Leaning closer, she cupped John's face in her hands and impulsively gave him a quick peck. *Oh my God, really?*

He looked at her questioningly.

She hesitated. *How can I ... I shouldn't ... I need to....* Her mind formed an apology, but before she could voice it, he leaned in and kissed her. All she could hear was the blood rushing in her ears.

They both sat silently for a moment, feeling the cool breeze on their faces. Bending his lips close to her ear, he whispered, "Thank you."

They rose from the sand and walked back toward the boardwalk.

"Wait a minute." Marjorie went back to the dune, found the driftwood, and ran back, carrying her treasure.

"You know, you never would have found that if it hadn't been for my driftwood detector," he said, indicating his injured toe.

"I guess that's true. How can I make it up to you?"

"Have breakfast with me?"

"I'd like that." They made it back to the boardwalk and parted with a friendly hug.

"I'll meet you at Victoria's at nine o'clock. Sound good?"

"See you there," she said as she turned up the street.

⚿

Early Sunday morning, Marjorie showered and dressed for her breakfast at Victoria's. Thanks to the sunshine, her face didn't require makeup. She packed the last of her things and walked down the steps to the lobby.

"Jillian?" she called. "I'd like to check out. I was also wondering if I could leave my bag here until after breakfast."

Jillian stuck her head out of the kitchen. "Of course, early bird. Sure thing. No coffee this morning?"

"No, thank you. Not this morning. I've been invited out, but I'm going down to the beach to do some writing first."

"Good for you. Before you leave, I just wanted to say you seem much happier. I don't mean to make you uncomfortable, but you look great."

"Truth is, I feel great, really great. Thanks for saying that. I needed this break more than I knew. It's been wonderful."

"Hey, have a great time. I'll see you when you pick up your bag."

Marjorie nodded. Grabbing her beach tote, she headed down to the water. She spread out the small towel and sat down. Taking out her notebook, she read:

> The beach. She is born with each sunrise and spends her hours mimicking human life. Thrust from darkness, with slices of light pushing through the dawn, she lies quietly. The rising sun governs the pace of her maturity. The breeze carries a hint

of cotton candy and caramel corn, mingled with shrieks of delight. The sun begins its slow drop. A sandcastle is wiped away, leaving a memory, and then not even that. She lives a lifetime in each new day. And the drifters return.

Marjorie read and re-read her entry. *She lives a lifetime in each new day.* She thought about the past two days at the Sea Sprite. They had sparked a vitality she hadn't felt for a long time, but the question she asked herself the first day still hadn't been answered. *What is it you are searching for, Marjorie?*

Her eyes scanned the water and the answer found her. She stood up and folded her towel, placing it in her tote along with her notebook and pen. Brushing the sand from her skirt, Marjorie walked toward the boardwalk. She passed Victoria's and smiled at the smell of breakfast sausage. Turning the corner, she filled her lungs with a deep, cleansing breath, certain she had made the right choice. As she stepped onto the verandah and opened the front door, Jillian practically ran over her.

"I'm so glad you're back. You didn't take your phone. I've been calling. Amanda's been calling."

Dread filled Marjorie. "What ... what is it?"

"It's Patrick," said Jillian, looking at Marjorie's stricken face. "No, he's fine. Don't worry, everything's fine."

"What is it? Please."

"Amanda called to tell you Patrick asked for you—by name. Marge, he's asking for you by name."

A sudden clarity filled Marjorie's thoughts. *I'm not sure how much time we have left, but whatever is left, I want to spend it with Patrick.* Marjorie turned and excitedly gathered her things. She was walking out the door when Jillian called out.

"Wait. Don't forget your driftwood."

"Keep it," she shouted back cheerily. "I've got to get home."

The table at Victoria's was set for two, a vase with fresh flowers centered between empty chairs. An hour after the nine o'clock reservation had passed, the table still waited. Both drifters had returned to familiar shores.

Jillian's Journal

August 23rd

I think I'm getting the hang of this thing. Marjorie's visit was not what I thought it would be. She didn't bring her husband, and it seemed to work out for the best. As they say, absence makes the heart grow fonder. I enjoyed having alone time with her, and it seemed like we could have become friends if she lived closer. I'm glad she was brave enough to come on her own. Watching her go through her own transition was a learning experience for me.

My takeaways?

One – I want to strive to be alive in each moment. What if something were to happen to me?

Two – When Chad and I were together, was there any point at which either of us could have influenced the decisions we each made? What will my future look like? Will I die alone? Marjorie's older than I am and she's fighting mediocrity. If she can triumph over it, I can, too. I think I will try to make a new habit of pursuing vitality. Tonight, I'll start with a bubble bath and a glass of Albariño.

The box: Casablanca tickets. They seemed to pull Marjorie in and flooded her with special memories. I wonder if it had anything to do with her rushing back to her husband. That kind of love, in Casablanca and between Marge and her husband—will I ever be so lucky?

THE LIGHTKEEPER

*J*illian often found herself outside after breakfast was finished. This morning, the muggy heat was already filtering through her shirt, pasting it to the skin of her back. A glass of lemonade and some soft tunes helped her relax. These moments were just what her weary bones needed.

Culling the burned-up summer flowers reminded Jillian it was time to renew the colors. She made a mental note to pick up some fall blooms for the pots. It might be worth checking the end-of-season sales for new seat cushions as well. Yellow was warm and wonderful, but a little change never hurt anyone—she was living proof.

Reinventing both herself and the Sea Sprite had given her hope. Jillian smiled to herself. Fuchsia cushions and yellow flowers for next year? It was something to consider. Sweat trickled down her face, and the heat rendered her incapable of any further serious thought.

She wiped her face on her sleeve to knock the sweat off. Goodness, if Grandma had seen her, it would have been the end of the world as she knew it. Luckily, Jillian was grown and used to making dozens of wrong decisions in record time. At least she held herself accountable and made sure she learned from each of them.

The stillness was ruined by the ringing of the reservation phone.

"Hello, are you on the way to relax at the Sea Sprite? This is Jillian. Can I help?" *That one was fun,* she thought.

"Ha. That's catchy, and yes, we are ready to visit."

"Great. Let's get you on the schedule," said Jillian.

"Perfect. I'm Karen. My boyfriend and I would like to make reservations for the twenty-fifth through the twenty-eighth, Thursday night through Monday morning."

Jillian was surprised to be getting a reservation call so early in the day. She was accustomed to getting calls in the late afternoon or evening. But things weren't always what they appeared to be, and people didn't always fit into the mold Jillian expected. She walked into the foyer and clicked her computer out of its slumber.

"We are looking forward to this. It's been too long since we've been away together," said Karen.

"Well, I'm hoping you'll have a great time here. Is there anything special I can help you with during your weekend?"

"Can you make sure there aren't any televisions, or electronic devices, or sporting events, or surfboards around?" Karen laughed. "Just kidding."

Jillian knew the things people joke about—most of the time—are an indication of the deepest truths. They finished up the reservation request and when Jillian hung up, she predicted a weekend at the Sea Sprite would be just what the couple needed.

⚷

"Oh, my God, no," shouted Karen. "You're going to drop me." Her blonde ponytail flipped in front of her youthful face.

Brody hoisted her 125-pound frame and carried her, laughing, across the verandah of the Sea Sprite. "Open the door, honey. I've got my hands full," he groaned in jest. "Hurry, please."

Karen reached out, grasped the handle, and pushed the door open. Brody stepped inside and bent his head for a kiss.

"Promise me," Karen said. "Promise me you'll love me forever."

"I promise." He brought his lips to hers again. Stepping through the door, they cautiously navigated past the seating area on the right. Two cozy glider rockers covered in white slipcovers rested on top of a colorful blue floral rug.

"Put me down over there," said Karen, nodding toward the chairs.

"Nope. Not ready to put you down yet."

They continued heading toward the reception area. Karen glanced around, taking in an old desk on the left of the casual stairway and center hall, and a large fireplace flanked by hundreds of books. Fresh bouquets of blue hydrangeas and colorful daylilies seemed to smile at them. There was no one in sight, but a pair of large double doors seemed to welcome a knock.

The next thing Karen knew, Brody was falling. Together, they tumbled to the floor in a heap.

"Wow, sorry about that," said Brody. "My foot must have caught the edge of the rug. Not very romantic."

"Good thing it's a thick rug."

"I may not be able to carry you, but I can love you."

Boy, isn't that the truth, thought Karen. *He does love me, but love alone doesn't build a future.*

"I will love you forever, you know."

Karen nodded; her eyes locked on his.

"I wish I could convince you I won't turn out like the rest of my family, Karen. I know I don't have my shit together yet, but I will—as soon as I get the trophy. I promise."

"Wait. You already promised. You're done with all that, right?"

"Oh, right. Repeat after me: We will get married, we will get married. . . ."

"I'm serious, Brody. Teaching yoga and meditation doesn't provide enough for us. If you want to move forward—like you say you do—I need you to show me, not tell me."

They heard footsteps coming down the stairs and looked up to see a woman with a concerned look on her face.

"I thought I heard a crash. Are you OK?"

"We made quite an entrance. Sorry you missed it," Karen said with a laugh.

Brody stood up and offered her a strong arm. "Here, babe, allow me."

"No way. That's what got me here in the first place." She took in his look, then reached for his hand and let him pull her to her feet.

"Sure you're OK?" asked the woman.

"Yup. Just fine, thanks. So we're Brody and Karen. I think our reservation is under Kasche," said Karen, realizing Brody's hand had made its way around to her rump.

"It's great to meet you. I'm Jillian, the owner."

"We're a little early," said Karen, delivering a behind-the-back swat to Brody's hand. "Would it be possible for us to check in?" Karen squirmed and finally grabbed the playful hand and held it pinned on the counter.

Jillian smiled. Looking at the computer screen she said, "Your room is ready."

"Oh, awesome," said Brody. "We may be able to make our picnic in Cape May tonight."

"Sounds wonderful," Jillian said, finishing the check-in on the computer.

"Actually, it's not just any picnic," explained Karen. "It's our four-year anniversary. On our first date, we had a picnic at the lighthouse, so we wanted to mark the occasion with another trip."

"How romantic," Jillian said, grabbing a set of keys from a rack behind the counter. "Let's get you up to your room so you aren't late."

After getting their things into the room, Karen returned to the lobby while Brody took a quick shower. She was looking at the old jewelry case when Jillian walked in from the kitchen. Responding to Karen's interest, Jillian told her the story of finding the old box and her search for the owner.

"What a lovely little locket," said Karen. "Do you know anything about it?"

"Only this," said Jillian, removing the locket from the case and opening it to show Karen.

The locket held a tiny black curl of hair. No longer than an inch, it had dulled over the years, but the deep-black pigment held true.

"I think it's probably a lock of hair from a baby worn close to a woman's heart, but unless I can find out who owned the box, I'll never know for sure."

"Actually, it looks more like the hair of an adult," said

Karen. "I might be wrong, but an infant's hair would be finer. Sorry—don't mean to sound like a know-it-all, but I work in the neonatal unit back home, so I see lots of baby hair. Maybe you could show it to someone else and get another opinion."

"No, now that I look at it, I think you may be right. Thanks. Any bit of information helps."

"Why do you care so much about finding the owner?"

"Great question. People are so tuned in to what they see in front of them. You know? Cellphones, laptops, televisions. All of it. But sometimes, the reality is much different than what we believe it to be. The more I learn about these little trinkets, the more I think they are leading me to someone's reality. I believe they were found for a reason, and I'm the person to get them back to their owner."

"That's so interesting. I wonder if it's the same with relationships. I mean, realities can be different, so sometimes things aren't what they seem."

"I think there are distractions in relationships. Sometimes they lead us to focus on a fake reality. If you can see the distractions I'm talking about, maybe your focus will move to a new reality."

Karen thought for a moment. "So how do you know if someone is *the one*?"

"I'm not sure. And I'm not the best person to ask. From what I've seen, you have someone who loves you very much. You just need to decide if that's what you are looking for."

Brody's aftershave showed up before him as he came down the stairs, showered and freshly shaven.

Karen let out a deep, frustrated sigh. Her eyes were focused on the front door of Obie's By the Sea, where Brody had disappeared ten minutes earlier to pick up their "romantic picnic." *Romantic picnic my ass,* thought Karen. *By the time we get to the lighthouse, it's going to be dark. We'll be lucky to finish without needing flashlights.*

She tried to help Brody focus on important details, but it didn't seem to be his nature. He went with the flow, whatever it was at the moment. He wasn't serious—ever. His party time, surfer-boy lifestyle was getting tiresome. She wanted to move to a deeper relationship, but she kept seeing signs that Brody might not be ready. Oh sure, he said he wanted a house, a family, a wife. He even went so far as to agree it was time to trade in the life of a surfer and yoga instructor for a full-time job with health benefits. But he hadn't submitted any applications. In fact, each time she asked Brody how he was doing with his resumé, the only three words she got were "working on it."

Karen knew what the problem was. But even though it stared her down, challenging her to validate its existence, she fought the reality. Years ago, her mom had taught her that love is a verb. Sitting here today, Mom's words seemed to echo in her brain. *Trust actions, Karen, never trust words. Words can lie. Actions always prove why words mean nothing.*

"All set?" Brody emerged from Obie's with a smile.

Karen struggled to swallow her anger while Brody bought the tickets for their ferry ride to Cape May. She wanted to make the most of it. This was the first year they could afford a vacation together, and she didn't want to ruin it. She had finally put her foot down and said, "No more surfing competitions. We can't afford it. This year is a vacation within driving distance; no surfing allowed." After weeks of debate, Brody had finally relented. He had not been pleased with the ultimatum, but at least he seemed to be taking her more seriously this time.

They left the car on the ferry's parking deck and headed upstairs to look around. "Yo, shipmate, you got yer sea legs yet?" Brody asked, grinning. "I need to head to the head, so if you'd be so kind as to pay for the booty?" He thrust his wallet toward her, wheeled about on his heel, and barked, "Then you take your landlubber self to the rails and keep a lookout. If you notice any commotion, you tell 'em to pipe down." Brody chuckled at his own joke, leaned in for a quick kiss, and commented, "Salty." Then he bounded toward the bathrooms, leaving Karen behind to pay for their matching sweatshirts.

Karen couldn't help being captivated by his positive energy and childlike enthusiasm. These were the traits she had fallen in love with.

Once the ferry docked, they drove their car off and headed to the Cape May lighthouse. After setting up a quiet spot, they sank onto the blanket, took out their plastic cups, and poured the wine.

"Wait, wait, wait." Brody grabbed her hand from the picnic basket and said, "I want to make a toast before we start eating."

Still holding his hand, Karen leaned back and looked into Brody's eyes. The message chime on Brody's phone broke the spell. He dropped her hand, pulled the cell out of his pocket, and glanced at it. *Really? You couldn't let it go?*

While he fiddled with his phone, Karen turned her focus to the basket. Thinking there would be some luscious appetizers and fruit under the lid, she peeked inside. She should have known better. Brody's idea of sexy food was lined up right on top: two Italian subs and matching bags of chips.

Brody clicked a few buttons and pushed the phone back into his pocket.

OK. Something is going on. Karen's stomach clenched.

"So my toast to you," Brody said, reaching for her hand.

Karen heard the phone ding in his pocket.

"Love isn't what makes the world go round." He paused for dramatic effect. "No, love is what makes our journey worthwhile."

Karen raised her cup and they bumped plastic. The phone dinged again, and Brody pulled it out to read the screen.

Finally fed up, Karen reached out and grabbed the phone.

"Hey! Give it back, it's nothing—just Frankie. Give it back." Brody reached for his phone and tried to jostle it away from Karen.

The text was from Frank: "Good luck, dude." Frank was Brody's partner in crime. Karen looked back at the thread. Brody had responded, "No. Going to later" in response to Frank's initial message, which was, "Did you tell her yet?"

"What do you have to tell me?"

"Well, I kind of wanted to wait 'till later to talk about it."

"No, let's talk about it now."

"OK. Frankie said he would help me, and I can pay him back the rest next month."

"What the hell are you talking about?"

"Umm ... the East Coast Surfing Championship in Virginia Beach." Brody's head dropped.

"Huh? Are you saying you're going to go surf in Virginia Beach? After we agreed no more surfing contests? Are you serious?"

"Yeah. I'm booked for September twenty-first through the twenty-eighth. I gotta do it."

Karen felt the air rush out of her. "But you promised."

"I know, baby, but I've got to do this one. I really think I've got a chance, and there's a lot of coin up for grabs. We could use it for a down payment on a house."

Karen stood. Shaking mad and in total silence, she started thrusting everything back into the basket. Brody—looking like a shamed child—reluctantly joined her. They bundled the unfinished picnic up and started heading toward the car.

Karen looked up and spotted an odd-looking shape at the base of the lighthouse. She thought it looked like a man holding a lantern on his outstretched arm, fast approaching the door. He swung the old lamp to and fro. Karen squinted, trying to make out the details, but she was too far away. His head seemed to swivel with each swing. She shivered, let out a gasp, and grabbed Brody's arm. The figure disappeared inside the lighthouse.

"Did you see that?" she yelled.

"What?"

"You didn't see him? The creepy guy with a lantern who just went into the lighthouse?"

"Nope, I didn't see anyone, but that's cool. They must be getting ready for a tour. Come on, let's go check it out."

"No. I'm staying right here. I told you, I don't even want to be around you right now."

"OK. I'll go see what's going on. It's probably just the lighting spooking you."

"I can't believe you're going in there."

"It's just a lighthouse. What's the big deal?"

"Never mind. Go."

"I'll be right back." Brody bounded toward the open door of the lighthouse. He waved to her before ducking inside.

Karen pulled out her flashlight and waited. She contemplated leaving him behind, but couldn't bring herself to do it. She could hear him calling out to someone. Standing alone, she thought about their relationship. Maybe she had pushed too hard. There was no sense in trying to convince someone that the time was right. It had to be right for both of them, or it would never work. Plus, how desperate would she be if she had to talk him into it? She was deep in thought when she heard him scream.

Their argument forgotten, Karen dropped the basket and raced to the lighthouse door. Yanking the door open, she squeezed through. "Brody?" Struggling in the dark, she tried to adjust her eyes.

"Karen!" he yelled. "Help, over here, help me."

The flashlight cut a narrow path of light in his direction. Karen ran to his side and gave him a once-over with the light. "Oh my God. What happened? Brody, you're hurt."

Pinning his left arm tightly to his side, Brody awkwardly tried to stand. Leaning on Karen, he moved toward the door with a pronounced limp.

"Did you see it?" His eyes darted back and forth madly; his head swiveled in each direction looking for something. "Did you?" Sweat ran in rivulets down his forehead and soaked through the armpits of his shirt.

With a firm grip on his clammy skin, Karen led him to the grass outside. "No, I didn't see anything. What was it?"

"You didn't see anything come out of the lighthouse? No

one?" White spit formed at the corners of his mouth.

"Brody, calm down, it's OK. Like you said, it's probably the lighting. You're outside now. It's over. Let's check you out first, and then we'll talk about it." Karen spoke calmly, trying to dampen his panic.

"No. We need to get out of here. Now."

"OK, let's move toward the car. Can you walk with me?"

Although Brody was limping, Karen didn't see any major injuries. He was holding his arm, but it didn't look broken. His face was banged up; blood was oozing slowly out of a small cut on his cheek. A large patch on his forehead was starting to swell. Karen guided him toward where she had been waiting. "We need to grab our picnic—"

"No!" Brody screamed. "We're leaving now. Forget about that stuff."

"All right," she said, trying to reassure him. "We'll go right now. Can you walk to the car?"

Brody was already limping toward the parking lot, his face pained. As soon as he was safely in the passenger side, Karen sat behind the wheel. Brody immediately reached for the button and locked the doors.

"Go," he demanded.

Karen started the car and headed back toward the ferry. Brody kept repeating, "Oh my God. Oh my God. What the hell?"

"You're scaring me. Please. Calm down and just talk to me."

"I don't know what I saw. I need a drink. A real drink. Turn toward town."

Karen spotted a sign for The Lush Lounge and swung

into the parking lot. It looked run-down, but she didn't want to waste time searching for something better. Turning off the ignition, she faced Brody. "Before we go in," she said, "let's talk for a minute. It looks like you hit your head. Do you remember falling?"

"Maybe I lost my balance. I feel OK. I just want a drink to help me calm down."

"All right. A quick one, but we should head back soon." She jumped out of the car and helped Brody. The limp was less noticeable, but he was still holding his left arm.

They walked straight to the bar and claimed a couple of mismatched stools with torn plastic seats. The bartender finished handing some change to a burned-out blonde at the end of the bar and casually walked over to Brody and Karen.

"Damn, looks like you guys have had a rough night and it's still pretty early."

"Jack on the rocks," Brody said abruptly. "Second thought, make it a double."

Karen spoke up, "I'll have a Jack and ginger, please. And, yes, it's been a rough night, but we're hoping you can make it better."

"OK. Be back with your drinks."

Karen kept her eyes on Brody. His breathing was still a bit ragged, and he was nervously picking at his fingernails. He absently ran his hands through his hair, held the back of his head, and buried his chin in the neckline of his shirt.

"Brody," Karen asked hesitantly, "can you tell me what happened?"

"I'm not sure what happened." Brody started. "I thought I saw this woman with a kid. I tried to talk to the old guy, but—"

"Slow down. Start from the beginning."

"When I went into the lighthouse, I glanced up the spiral staircase and followed the glow. When I got to the first landing, I yelled out, 'Is it cool if I come up?' You know, so I wouldn't scare anybody. I heard boots climbing higher, so I yelled 'Hello?' louder. The noise stopped."

"You think he just didn't hear you?"

"I did think maybe he was a little hard of hearing. Then when I got to the first landing, the air changed. First it was dry and dusty, then it got like ... I don't know, like nasty basement air. It was cold and smelly. I didn't hear anyone come into the lighthouse, but when I turned around, it looked like there was a woman about five steps down from me who was carrying a kid."

"Wait, she was behind you? But you didn't see her when you went in?"

"Look, the light was weird. Maybe I was wrong. I thought it was light from his lantern, but then I saw light coming in through the windows. Looked like she was wearing a white dress. Really weird. Next thing I knew, she was gone."

The bartender showed up with their drinks and set the glasses down. Karen looked up to see him send a wink to someone across the room, then turned her attention back to Brody.

"So I ran up the steps, yelling for help. I must have yelled three times. When I got to the second landing, I saw the outline of a man under the window. It really pissed me off that he didn't answer me, so I screamed at him, 'Did you see someone else in here?' Then he just kind of shifted. I heard this loud 'whoosh' and he disappeared."

"Here," said Karen, pushing his whiskey toward him,

"drink some of this. Was it really a man, or was it the lights?"

"I don't know what it was."

Brody was visibly shaking. Karen rested her hand on his shoulder in support. "It's all right; you're fine now."

"It's not all right. I'm not fine. Look, I was standing there, sweating from running up the steps. Then I saw it again, but this time, it was moving really fast, like jerking back and forth. I hauled ass down to the first landing. I looked back up the stairs, but when I did, I felt this huge blast of cold air and lost my balance. I guess that's when I fell down the stairs."

Brody's voice had grown louder and louder as he recalled the story. The bartender was keeping a close eye on the two of them. When Brody's volume reached its highest, the man walked back over.

"Sorry to intrude, but it's my job to ask. Everything OK here?" He stood with his hands gripping the counter.

Brody picked up his drink and drained it. He pushed the empty glass back to the bartender and said, "Another."

"Yes, I think everything's OK," answered Karen. "We just had something really strange happen at the lighthouse. We're a little shaken up over it."

The bartender retreated to fill Brody's request.

"You guys aren't from around here, are you?" asked the bartender as he set Brody's refill in front of him.

"No. We're staying in Rehoboth and came over to picnic," Karen said.

"Well, if you want to know more about the lighthouse, you're in luck. See the guy in the far corner?" He nodded his head toward the dark table where a large man sat with his back against the wall.

"Yes. Who is he?" asked Karen.

"That's Mack. Short for McCallister. Captain McCallister. You two need to talk to him." He put two fingers in his mouth and whistled. "Hey, Mack. Talk to these two about the lighthouse."

Mack raised his huge hand and waved them over.

"Come on, Brody," Karen said. "Let's go see what he knows."

Brody grabbed his newly filled drink and followed Karen.

Mack was a huge man. His body spilled over both sides of the chair. A dark cable-knit turtleneck showed from beneath a denim shirt littered with small rips and holes. His jeans fared no better. They were worn off at the cuff, and the ends had grated off, leaving behind a white, soft fiber fringe. Most of his black belt was smothered under his fleshy middle. He kicked out the chairs across from him, sending them back from the table about a foot. Karen surmised this was Mack's gesture of welcome. She slid into the farthest one and scooted closer. Brody followed suit. Mack grabbed the half-full bottle of Jack Daniels from the table and filled his glass. Lifting it, he nodded at Brody, who grabbed his in response. The two men raised their glasses and looked at Karen with expectant eyes. Karen joined the toast.

Mack's nose disappeared into the cup. He lifted it higher to drain every drop. His dancing eyes peeked over the rim, and Karen could have sworn Mack winked at her. He slammed his glass down on the table and grabbed the bottle again. This time, he reached across and filled Brody's glass first.

"So you two were out at the lighthouse, were ya?" he started.

"Yes," said Brody, "we were there. What can you tell us about the place?"

"Not so fast there, beach boy. Why don't ya fill me in on what happened while you were there."

Brody led Mack through his terrifying tour of the lighthouse. He replayed every step he had taken, everything he saw, and every word he had spoken. He didn't stop there. He detailed everything he smelled, felt, or heard while he was inside the building. Mack nodded and occasionally grunted. He urged Brody to share more with a nod of his head.

Mack's leathery face appeared expressionless. His droopy lower eyelids were wet and hung slightly disconnected from his eyes. Finally, he raised his right eyebrow—the one with a scar running through it—and spoke.

"This here is nuthin' new." Mack sat back in the chair and laced his fingers over his belly, as if protecting the investment, and continued. "Fact is, I can't count the folks who have come to me with a story like yers over the years. So don't feel lucky. Happens a lot."

At this, Brody scoffed, "Yeah, I feel lucky, all right. Real lucky."

Mack didn't acknowledge the interruption. Instead, he continued. "Caleb was the lightkeeper from 1903 to 1924. Those years were tough ones 'round here. Either of ya heard of the Spanish flu?"

Both Brody and Karen shook their heads silently.

"Nah, not many people these days think much of the influenza. Hell, all ya do is run into the local 'Spend More Greens' drug store, get a free poke in yer arm full of watered-down bugs, and ya never have to worry 'bout bein' sick. But let me tell ya 'bout what happened here in 1918. Spanish

Influenza dropped fifty million people. Hell, we only lost sixteen million in World War I. Death came over on the boats when the war was still goin' heavy. We had a whole bunch of military boys 'round here, and most said they carried the death home with 'em never knowin' it." Mack paused to refill both glasses of Jack. He raised the bottle toward Karen, but she was content to sip on hers slowly.

"The doctors? Hell, not a one of 'em knew their onions. It killed healthy folks mostly—forty and younger, some real young—would turn up their blood to a hundred 'n' six degrees. Their skin would go dark. Jest as soon as that happened, blood would start jest a pourin' outta their noses like they got clobbered. Some of 'em died real quick. Others got jest a bit better for a day or two. Then the damn devil would come back and fill up their lungs with water 'till they drowned. It was ugly."

"But what does this have to do with the lighthouse?" Karen asked.

"Well, doll, jest a little bearcat, ain't ya?" Mack snickered. "Hold yer lacy parts and I'll git there. Seems like ya ought a finish that drink, stead a nursin' it all night. Maybe that'd take a bit a starch outta ya."

Karen spun her head to face Brody, but he was focused on every word Mack was saying. She wasn't about to get any support at this table. She decided to oblige the old coot and drained her drink.

"That's a girl," Mack encouraged. "So. Old Caleb, the lightkeeper, he and his wife were thrown into a shitstorm when their daughter up and died with seven little ones at home. His assistant lightkeeper was out helpin' other people. As the books tell it, the streets in town? They was piled hip-high with rottin' flesh. One undertaker to shoot 'em all full a some special potion that kept 'em pickled till they got back to their families. He couldn't keep up with the grim reaper. People in town walked their kids down different streets to keep the young'uns from seein' all them stacks of death."

"Jesus." Karen reached for the bottle of Jack and helped herself.

"Oh yes. I imagine His name shot across a lot a lips durin' them dark days. So here's Caleb, tryin' his damnedest to find a replacement to run the lighthouse so they can go say good-bye to their beloved daughter 'fore she's buried. Then they needed to take care a her babies, to try to keep the rest of 'em clean from the flu. But there's no replacement to be found. So he sends for the only other person he knows can handle the lighthouse—his big brother, Aaron.

Caleb knew Aaron would help him. Aaron never said no to nuthin', even when it meant extra hardship. So, o' course, Aaron showed up to help, along with his bride, Hannah, and their young son, Abraham."

"Look," Karen said. "This is all very interesting, but this happened in, what did you say, 1918? Can you move this story along to the present?"

For the first time during the conversation, Brody piped up. "Chill out, Karen. Let the man finish. Just because—like me—he doesn't fit exactly in your schedule doesn't mean it's necessarily a bad thing."

"Are you kidding me?" Karen's chest and neck flushed defensively. "Did you just try to spin this conversation into a relationship thing?"

"Looks that way."

"We wouldn't even have been arguing if you'd kept your

word about not competing anymore. But no, you had to sign up for another competition without telling me. You haven't sent out one resume in six months. How are we supposed to get a house when you don't even get paid regularly?"

"Look, let's forget it. We can hash all this out again later. Let the man finish."

"So as I was sayin'," said Mack, "Aaron, Hannah, and Abraham hunkered down at Caleb's place. It was only supposed to take a few days, but the third week takin' care of them babies and son-in-law was jest as bad as the first for Caleb and his wife. Aaron took almost all a the lighthouse shifts, leaving only from midnight to four each night to join his family in the lightkeeper's cottage.

"The way the story has passed down, one night there was a knock-down, drag-out fight between Aaron and his wife. Hannah told Aaron he was neglectin' his family. Aaron told her he had to do what he had to do and returned to the lighthouse. There was a storm that night, and Aaron had to stay at the lighthouse to signal the ships. When mornin' came, the lighthouse assistant found Aaron's wife and child on the road, dead. It was a real dark scene. It looked like they had been in the lighthouse durin' the storm. Aaron was at the top—probably outside tendin' the light—and never heard them. There was no way they could a climbed all them steps in that condition. They were likely on the way back home when they died. Poor souls."

"Oh my God," Karen whispered, her face pinched into a grimace. "What a horrible story."

"Yeah, it sure was," Mack added. "Guess they found a rattle on the landin', so they knew she had lugged the young'un up the steps, but she couldn't find Aaron. She was too weak to make it the rest of the way. She took the boy back downstairs and tried to reach the cottage. She exhausted herself, and the sickness passed through both of 'em with wicked speed. Probably took on a fit of the coughin', fell down, and just couldn't get up again."

"So wait—you're saying you think I ran into Aaron and Hannah?" Brody's eyes were wide.

"I'm jest sayin' it's possible. Aaron and Hannah have been tryin' to find each other for almost a hundred years. He died sittin' next to their headstones over in Cold Spring Cemetery. Most people think it was a broken heart."

"Wow," Karen whispered. "They must still be in love after all this time."

"Now yer on the trolley," Mack boomed. His last grab of the bottle filled all three of their glasses with a single shot. Lifting his, he cheered, "To eternal love. May those who have it recognize it while they still walk the earth." His crooked sausage fingers set the empty glass down carefully on the table.

Brody and Karen looked at each other. Neither of them spoke while they processed Mack's story. A run-in with ghosts? Hundred-year-old ghosts?

"Nah. I don't believe it," said Brody. "I'll admit I was spooked there for a bit, but that's not real. He's making it up. It's like local lore you use to scare all the tourists, right?"

Mack sucked his teeth with his tongue like he was wishing he had a toothpick, but he didn't answer Brody.

"Maybe, but don't forget, I saw something, too," said Karen. "Mack, that's quite a story. How do you know all this?"

Mack leaned over the table and whispered. "Caleb was my great, great, grandpa. My grandma was one a them seven wee ones that lost their momma."

"Wow," Karen said. "Thanks for sharing the story."

"Yup, sure 'nough. I've got a few more things I'm feelin' the need to share with ya two hard-headed youngsters, so maybe ya have a chance of figurin' yerselves out before it's too late."

"We're fine," said Brody, "but thanks for trying to help."

"No, Brody," Karen interjected. "I don't think we are fine. I want to hear what Mack has to say. Don't you? What was it you said to me earlier? Let the man finish. Just because he doesn't fit exactly in your schedule doesn't mean it's a good idea to run out."

"So ya wanna hear my little jeweled nuggets?" asked Mack.

Brody nodded his agreement.

"First off is honesty. Ya both need to be honest 'bout everythin'. What yer history's about, what ya think right now, and what ya see on the road ahead. This gives a real picture to both a ya kids 'bout who ya really were, who ya are, and what ya want." Mack paused. The only reaction he got was Brody and Karen looking at each other.

He continued. "Two, there's such a thing as a happy bank. If ya wanna good bond, ya gotta make as many happy bank deposits as ya can and try not to make withdrawals. A man and a woman gotta figure out how to make each other happy—and how to stop makin' each other crazy."

"Makes sense," Brody acknowledged with a small smile. "Like I should stop doing the stuff I know makes her crazy and do more things I know get me brownie points."

"Yeah, beach boy. Catchin' on, ain't ya," said Mack, while a grin spread over his grizzled cheeks. "Lucky I'm tellin' ya this before it's too late. Sure wish I still had my Maggie. We learned all this together. Third marriage fer both of us, but this one was the right one. That's what I know fer sure."

"I'm sorry you don't have her anymore," Karen said quietly.

"Yup, the world's a darker place without her sunshine in it." Mack paused a few seconds. "Number three is the most important one of all. Number three is total agreement. This here means ya never—and I mean never—do anythin' without total agreement. Ya got it? It means if there's somethin' ya want and she doesn't, or somethin' she wants and ya don't—if either of 'em's the choice, ya do nothin'. Decisions gotta be one hundred percent agreed on. From here on out, no decidin' on yer own what the right thing is to be doin'. From now on, ya both decide together. And if ya can't? Ya do nuthin'."

"Dude, that's some really positive shit right there," Brody said.

"Thank you," Karen said. "I feel like between your words and the story of Aaron and Hannah, we've got a lot to think about." Mack winked at her again. This time she had no doubt—she caught his wink in action.

"Indeed ya do. Don't wait till yer time's up before ya figure it all out. You two get on outta here. Good luck to ya."

Just like that, they were excused from the private little table where they had learned the secrets to a good life. As they walked out the door, both of them laughed as they heard a quick whistle and Mack shouting out, "One more fer the road. I gotta toast my Maggie."

They walked toward the car, and Brody cautiously reached for Karen's hand.

"I'm sorry, Karen. Forgive me?"

"How's your arm?"

"It's fine. But if you don't mind, it would feel better around you."

Karen reluctantly slid under his arm. They were wrapped up, separately processing the details from Mack's conversation. Karen heard Brody's phone ding with another text. She presumed it was Frankie again, wanting to know how she reacted to the news. Brody reached into his pocket and the screen lit up. He touched it a couple of times and brought the phone to his ear.

"Hey, Frankie. Yeah, so I've changed my mind about going to Virginia Beach."

Karen could tell the response was animated. Although the words were mumbled, she did catch "whipped" since Frankie practically yelled it. *Nice,* she thought. Whatever his reason, she was really happy to see Brody actually take action.

"Think what you want, Frankie. It was my decision. I've just been fooling myself, pretending I can play my whole life and get by. But I learned some things tonight that I damn sure don't want to forget." Brody ended the call and turned to look at Karen.

He started quietly, "I'm real sorry, Karen. I promised you I'd love you forever and I meant it. I guess I just wasn't ready to be an adult; that's why I did all that selfish stuff. But after this crazy night? I know we've got what it takes to make it— if we do it together. I don't want to search for you forever. I want you with me. I'm willing to do what it takes. Will you help me?"

"We can help each other." Karen sighed, her lips gently grazing his cheek. "Like you said, love isn't what makes the world go round. Love is what makes the journey worth it, and we've got a lifetime to figure it out."

Jillian's Journal

August 28th

It was so interesting this weekend to watch people try to determine what is real and what isn't. There are so many distractions from what's "real" in life. It was so obvious to me that Brody was totally in love with Karen, and yet, she didn't see it. Maybe he didn't even see it—too busy searching for the elusive trophy to see that what really matters is right in front of him. Of course, Chad was cheating on me and stealing from the firm, and I never saw it. I pay much closer attention to things today.

My takeaways?

One – My life used to be full of distractions: friends who were really just acquaintances, a career that kept me too busy to enjoy my life, fancy cars, a big boat, an expensive house, and to make it shiny, a bunch of meaningless jewelry. I need to be mindful of what I let in. Never forget what's real.

Two – The surfing did sound like fun. Note to self: put it on the calendar.

The Box: Still waiting for the trinkets to talk to me. When Karen pointed out the locket, I remembered the tiny clippings I still have of Maegan's baby hair. I was sure this locket held the same treasure, but she was adamant it held the hair of an adult. Only the most intense love would prompt someone to think of inviting a tiny curl to rest on their heart. So who does the hair belong to?

BEYOND THE DUNES

*L*abor Day. Jillian took a long drink of ice water. She couldn't believe Labor Day was almost here. Only last year, she was out on the boat with her family, pulling an inner tube filled with kids. Back then, her life was defined by the people surrounding her. This year, she had decided no one would make her changes for her. She held the power to succeed or fail. The things she used to identify as important now had little meaning. She strove to be an accomplished survivor of her former life. She was replacing shallow relationships with those that had deep foundations. In permanent ink, she was rewriting her future by working hard to be joyfully present every day. "Why wait?" became her signature line, and practicing it had transformed her. Jillian wondered what the world held in store for her now.

Evidently, it was a new guest, she thought, as she reached to answer the ringing phone.

"Hi, it's the Sea Sprite and this is Jillian. Summer's almost over; are you coming to stay with us?" *I kind of like playing this by ear,* she thought.

"Oh."

"Does that mean you're thinking about it?" joked Jillian. "I'm sorry. I try to be a little silly when I answer the phone. Gets me into a lot of trouble. This is Jillian, and I run the Sea Sprite. Can I help you with something?"

"Oh, right." A little giggle eased its way through the signal. "You caught me off guard. So, yes. I'm thinking about coming to the beach for Labor Day weekend, but I need to ask a few questions."

"OK, ready when you are. Shoot."

"Do you have any pets in the facility?"

"Pets? No, we don't have any pets. I do have a few friendly hummingbirds that like to hang out with the guests in the yard, but the only living creatures inside the Sea Sprite are the humans. Well ... that I know of, anyway."

OK. Do you have Wi-Fi? And if you do, is there a charge for it, or a usage limit?"

"Yes, there is Wi-Fi, and it's free for paying guests and their visiting friends. Unlimited bandwidth. Did you like that? I just threw 'unlimited bandwidth' out there. I'm not really sure what I have, but I heard it on a commercial and it sounded good. I can find out for you, though."

"Technically, there is bandwidth speed and bandwidth capacity. Bandwidth speed depends on the network, your computer, and even the speed of the server at the other end. It's not likely you have unlimited bandwidth capacity. The truth is, even the providers don't have unlimited bandwidth, so they can't offer it to the end user."

"Wow. I never would have known." With a silent roll of her eyes, Jillian thought, *and I never would have needed to know it, either.*

She finished the reservation and interview process. Emma would be staying for the weekend. *Based on the phone call,* Jillian thought, *Emma might be in need of a transformation of her own.*

Emma threw her phone across the room and onto the bed. It skied across a shiny comforter too fancy to be practical. The last of its ride was spent skidding off the far side of the bed—the bed she hadn't even had a chance to sit on before she got the call.

"Damn it!" Her ears felt hot. She replayed the conversation in her mind, just to make sure it was as bad as she thought it was.

"I know you are supposed to be off, but the system went down. No emails coming in or going out. We can't even email in-house. Do you know how busy we are this weekend?"

Emma remained silent. Blood pulsed in her ears. She had arrived at the Sea Sprite less than an hour ago, and now they expect her to drive all the way back to King of Prussia?

"Come on, Emma. I realize you're on vacation, but you'll have plenty of time to relax when you get back, won't you?" Blah, blah, blah.

Bitch, thought Emma, *I wonder if punching you in the face would be worth losing my job.* "Yes" was the easy answer. Funny thing was, no one would ever suspect Emma had the ability to morph into a demon bitch from hell. Granted, the morphing only took place in her mind, but it was still a worthy alter ego.

"Well? Are you coming? Hello? Are you?" Regina's pleading, nasally whine was like fingernails on a blackboard to Emma.

"I'll consider it." Emma felt her demon bitch persona losing ground, and she hurled the phone across the room. The phone started ringing from the floor. She bent down to retrieve it and glanced at the caller ID. *Oh great. Now, it's Paul.*

Paul had been Emma's boss at the IT consulting firm for ten years. He had not only been willing to overlook her awkwardness with people—she knew her technical skills made up for it—he had also welcomed her into his family. She was often invited for dinner or to spend holidays with them. Emma even loved their rambunctious labradoodle, Snickers, despite the sneezing, runny nose, and itching that resulted from her pet dander allergy. This was why she could never turn Paul down when he asked. He was the one who insisted she take off for the weekend, claiming there was no need for her to stay in the shop. *Sure there wasn't.*

"Hello, Paul," said Emma, answering the phone with a groan.

"Sheesh, kid, don't sound so damn depressed. I wouldn't be calling if it weren't an emergency."

"So instead of a weekend at the beach, I have to deal with the crows at the Bitchy Team?"

"It's Vicchy Team, and I don't like Regina Vicchy any more than you do, but her realty company is one of our biggest clients."

"I never should have brought my phone with me."

"I'll pay for your weekend to be extended to a whole week if you can rescue us." She could picture his shoulders drooping, his head tipped downward, and his pleading eyes begging for her help.

"First," she said, "you're going to owe me big time. Second, you throw in gas, tolls, and mileage. Last, make sure when I show up, the crows are out of the office. I don't feel like wasting time with them, and the only reason I'm doing this is because you asked."

Emma whisked up her laptop and stuffed it into the

satchel. She returned to the lobby of the Sea Sprite, where Jillian was perched at the desk with a red bandanna in one hand and a small mason jar in the other.

"Hey Emma," Jillian called out, "what do you think of these for the barbecue tomorrow?"

Emma gave it a quick glance. "So clever. I would never think of something so artsy." Several mason jars were stuffed with bandannas of red, white, and blue. In the center of each one, Jillian had placed a set of eating utensils.

"Oh, don't give me too much credit," said Jillian. "I spotted it on Pinterest, and by some stroke of luck, I was able to save it. I haven't really figured out Pinterest. It's nice to be a little festive on special days. If people are happy, hopefully they'll want to come back."

"I could teach you how to use Pinterest if we had more time. Matter of fact, I'd like to know if it would be possible to extend my stay through the end of the week? I know it's late notice, but my boss gave me a little extra vacation time."

"I could use some computer help, that's for sure. The rest of the week is open, if you want to stay. It's my first season, so reservations have been a little sporadic." Jillian thought back to her first guest, Carol, and smiled to herself. "Matter of fact, maybe we can make a deal. If you show me a few things on the computer, I'll give you a discount."

"Sounds perfect. You ever get tired of trying to make other people happy?" asked Emma with a sigh.

"Believe me, there are days when I don't think I'll ever get it right. I do like to give people a special place where they can be happy—if they choose. But I try really hard not to rely on other people for my satisfaction. I've learned to validate myself based on how well I execute my own plans. I find it empowering."

"Wow." Emma paused. "I'm going to think about that on my way back to work."

"Back to work?"

"Yep. Haven't even unpacked, and now I have to head back to work. So I'll either be back tonight, or early tomorrow morning."

"Got it. If you're back in time, you're welcome to join me and a few of my friends who are coming over to decorate for the party. It should be a lot of fun."

"It's not really my thing, but thanks for the invite. I'll keep it in mind."

Emma squeezed herself in behind the wheel, put her bubble gum and dark chocolate Raisinets close enough to reach, and plugged her cell into the charger. She had a three-hour drive back to King of Prussia and wanted to be sure she had enough fuel to recharge herself on the road.

She spent the drive evaluating her life. Ever since she graduated from college, Emma tried to find ways to blend in. Thirteen years later, she still hadn't figured out the formula.

She walked in the front door of the Vicchy Team's office at three o'clock. As promised, it was empty. By five, she had solved the crisis and was back in her car, heading south to the Sea Sprite—for the second time.

This time, she was excited. After reviewing her life, she decided she was lacking passion and needed to find some. She wanted something to give her a purpose, not just a paycheck. It would help her fit in and feel part of a bigger picture. It was going to be tough since the only thing she was passionate about was her work. She was so focused on her career path, she really had no clue about how to find a new hobby. She would have to give it some thought.

It was getting dark when Emma pulled back into the driveway of the Sea Sprite, but the inn was lit up and inviting. There was a lively trio of women unpacking the car next to hers.

Emma took a deep breath. "Hi ladies. Need an extra hand with those boxes?"

"Well, of course, honey. Come on over and give us a hand. I'm afraid we might have gone a little overboard with stuff for the party."

Emma smiled at the tiny senior citizen with pink streaks in her hair.

"I'm Barb, Jilly's next door neighbor. This is Amy, her best

friend, and the tall blonde here is Greta."

"So nice to meet all of you." Emma awkwardly tried to shake hands at the same time Barb was stacking decorations in her arms.

"Your timing is spot on," said Amy. "Let's go see what's in store for us."

Inside, Jillian reintroduced everyone. Amy walked over to the registration desk and plopped down a huge box with sides rounded by overstuffing.

"Geez," said Jillian, "how many people do you think are going to be here for the barbeque?"

Both Barb and Greta were weighted down with more bags than anyone should carry at once.

"Hey, the foyer looks amazing. Love the desk," said Amy.

"It's the same one I've had since we opened; nothing new."

"Do you realize I haven't been in this room since I showed up with Brad for your renovation estimate?"

"That's not possible. My God, you're here all the time. At least it seems like it to me," Jillian teased.

Barb chimed in, "I believe it. When I see her here, she's always in the kitchen, or in the backyard with a beer."

"Just like your little sign says," Greta reminded, "backdoor guests are always best."

"It's so true," said Amy. "I guess I really haven't been around here much. You stayed with us during the renovation, and you still hang out at Mom's bakery on Sundays. We have plenty of time together—way more than I want." Amy started laughing at her own joke.

"OK, enough with the funny stuff. Let's get this place decorated," said Greta. "Here, you take these flags out back and start hanging them up." She handed a box to Amy.

"Fine. You guys are just trying to get rid of me. I'll start out back all by myself." Amy winked and sauntered down the hallway toward the kitchen.

"Hey, this is a really cool piece," said Greta, looking at the display case. "Where did you get it?"

"Oh," said Jillian. "I bought it at the auction. It's an antique jewelry case. Isn't it great? Remember the box of stuff I told you guys about? The one the contractor found under the floorboards upstairs? I've been displaying it in there until I figure out who it belongs to."

"Oh, right. Have you connected any dots yet?"

"I've had a few guests who have helped. A young lifeguard found a picture of the same girl hanging in his church, so I found her first name. I just don't know how to put it all together, or even how to research it. You know me;

I'm not internet-savvy. Emma, maybe you can help me out? I'd really like to find the owner and give it back. I'll admit, I'm a little obsessed with it."

Emma wandered over to look. "This sure is intriguing; sounds like a fun project."

Greta laughed. "Solving the mystery would be fun, but I'm not so sure I envy you trying to turn Jilly into a techie."

⚷

The next morning, Emma rolled out of her bed at the Sea Sprite. She packed her rolling beach bag, contemplating each addition. *Steve Jobs*—the book she had been trying to read all year—was first on the list. A nice, fluffy beach blanket, a small towel she could roll up under her neck, and snacks followed. Lots of snacks. Impulsively, she grabbed the complimentary Sea Sprite journal from the top of her dresser and tossed it in with a pen to capture an epiphany, should one occur.

Emma drove to Cape Henlopen looking for the quiet beaches Jillian had mapped out for her. She thought every last inch of the sand would be occupied—especially Labor Day weekend—but she was able to find a stretch of beach that was nearly empty. Dry white sand stretched in front of her. Dunes were topped off by mounds of seagrass whose wiry fingers swayed in the breeze, making them look lush and soft.

Clouds slowly glided across the blue expanse of sky, and sea gulls swooped overhead, complaining loudly. Emma passed a sign indicating a nesting area for endangered birds. The only other people nearby were a group of young, shirtless men who were taking turns throwing a football to each other. Emma tugged the unwieldy beach bag through the sand to its final resting spot. Surveying the view, she decided it was a great spot to perch. Watching a group of guys throw a ball around would likely provide some entertainment if she needed a break from her book. They were close, but not too close.

Holding the beach blanket at two corners, Emma lifted it up and let the wind unfurl it. Laying it flat, she tucked each corner underneath itself with a pocket of warm sand to hold it down. As she did on her road trips, she arranged her snacks in order of preference. It was important for her to have her favorite snacks closest. Peanut M&M's were first. Next were the Twizzlers and Necco wafers—they tied for second place—and almost beyond her reach, where they belonged, were the baby carrots. In Emma's life, natural foods rarely got the attention they deserved. Her sweet tooth always trumped her desire to be healthier.

She opened the Sea Sprite journal and grabbed her first handful of M&M's. After pondering a few moments, Emma began to list out her new strategy.

1. Make new friends
2. Help someone who has a special need
3. Identify an interest

The more she wrote, the more inspired Emma became. She was beginning to see opportunities in places she had never thought of before. *Look at me,* she thought. *This is just like troubleshooting at work.* Jillian's words came back to her: "I've learned to validate myself based on how well I execute my own plans. I find it empowering." For the first time in years, Emma could see herself participating in some of the activities she had conjured up, surrounded by new people.

"Heads up!" yelled a male voice. "Look out!"

Emma raised her eyes from her work and watched the football fly over her head and land with a heavy thud somewhere in the dunes behind her. The guy who had thrown it jogged in her direction. Emma couldn't help but think of him as "Mr. Matchy." Everything he wore was the exact same shade of royal blue, even his flip-flops.

"Uh, sorry for disturbing you," he mumbled as he ran past.

"It's OK," Emma said, after a moment's hesitation.

"Yo, Gary," Mr. Matchy called from the dunes behind her. "We got a problem."

"Dude," Gary responded. "You can't throw *and* you can't see? Is that the problem?" The entire group of guys laughed.

"Seriously, the ball hit a bird," he said.

At this news, Emma's stomach clenched. *Oh no*, she thought. *Poor bird. They shouldn't have been playing so close to the nesting area.*

Another one of the boys sauntered over. "Hey, Gary, it's not dead, but it's hurt." He yelled over the top of Emma. "What should we do?"

Gary swore and then said, "Well, you can't leave it there."

"I guess we should put it out of its misery. I'll go get the water jug and we can crush it. Or you think we should drown it? Which is better?"

"I've got a hammer in my truck. It would be fast, but might be messy."

Emma's startled intake of air broadcast her alarm. She craned her head around and stared at them. She wavered but realized if she didn't intervene, these guys were going to "off" the poor bird. She stood and marched toward them through the sand.

"You're kidding, right?" she asked them hopefully. "You aren't seriously going to kill an injured bird, are you?"

She was met with stammers and sheepish glances at the sand.

"You've got to be kidding me."

"Look," said Mr. Matchy, "it's not like we wanna hurt the bird. We just want to put him out of his misery so he's not in pain. My dad says that's the best thing to do in situations like this."

"Oh, I see. So then it's OK with your dad if we decide to smash your head in with a hammer when you break an arm? After all, you won't be in pain anymore, so it's OK, right?" Emma sighed deeply. Her face was red, and her short, unpolished nails dug into her palms, leaving pink crescent indentations.

For the first time, she looked down and saw the bird. She lost all of the angry steam she had built up and knelt near the tiny bird. Its cottony, white belly was perched on top of two oversized orange stilts, one of which was bent at an odd angle. "Guys, this really isn't good. I think this is a piping plover. It's an endangered species." She was met with silence.

Emma's eyes filled with tears as she assessed the injured bird. His little orange beak looked like the tiny tip was dipped into an inkwell, and he had a comical black uni-brow over his eyes. A band of black circled his neck like a formal bow tie. As if the circumstances weren't difficult enough, his right wing was also fully extended and hung from his side. His tiny, expressive eyes looked at Emma calmly while she evaluated the situation. It didn't take long for her to process a workaround in her head. She was used to finding solutions when none were apparent.

"I've got this," she told the boys. "Go over to my blanket and bring me the little towel. I'm going to find someone to help him." When they returned with the towel, she told them to go back over and pack up her things in the wheeled cart—hard stuff on the bottom, soft stuff on top—while she approached the bird.

Emma carefully wrapped the injured bird in the small towel. Nervous perspiration covered her face. Her shaking hands finished the job as she silently prayed. *Please, don't let me hurt the little guy.* She walked over to the roller bag with the bird in her hands and tucked it into the folds of the blanket, leaving plenty of breathing room.

"Thanks for doing this. We didn't mean to hurt him."

Emma's face softened. "I know it was an accident. I hope you move a little farther from the nesting area. And next time you see an injured animal and it needs you, try your best to help. My dad told me being kind doesn't cost you anything, especially when it comes to those who can't help themselves. Plus, just trying to help will make you feel way better at the end of the day." She grabbed the handle of the roller bag and started struggling to get it through the sand.

"Here, let us help." Mr. Matchy and his quiet friend each took a side of the bag carefully and lifted it. Together, they walked it all the way back to her car and put it safely inside.

"That was really nice, you guys. Go enjoy the rest of your day. No worries. This little guy is in good hands." Emma wasn't so sure she was telling the truth, but she was going to try her best.

Sliding behind the steering wheel, she said to her new feathered friend, "Geez, seems like I'm destined to spend my entire vacation in a car. Well, let's find you some help, buddy."

Before starting the car, Emma decided she needed a plan. *I'm pretty great at troubleshooting, so let me think for a minute. Plan A: How do I solve this?* "Oh, I know," she said out loud, "the sign probably had a contact number on it." Emma ran back with her journal to jot down the number, but there was none listed. *OK—moving to Plan B.*

Emma pulled out her cellphone and punched "Delaware bird rescue" into her search engine. The first listing that popped up was Beach Bird Rescue. Thankfully, their website had a link titled, "Help, I Found an Injured Bird." The page had a phone link on it, so Emma clicked on it. The friendly woman who answered confirmed that Emma's bird was probably a plover and thanked her profusely. She told Emma to get the bird into a cardboard box with plenty of air holes and said a wildlife rehabilitator would be in contact with her. Emma breathed a sigh of relief.

She had the whole process outlined in her head now. She called Jillian and explained her plover rescue mission and what was needed. When she arrived at the Sea Sprite, an empty cardboard box was waiting on the reception desk. Ventilation holes had already been made.

"Will that work?" Jillian asked, walking in from the kitchen.

"I think so. He's pretty small, so he'll have plenty of room. Thanks for fixing it up. Now, I just need to get him out of this." She pointed to the roller bag.

Emma opened the bag slowly while Jillian watched. There, on top, was the little bird wrapped in a towel. Emma reached in and gently lifted the bird. She walked toward the box on the desk, holding the bird gingerly. As she raised her hands over the desk, the bird started to struggle. His frenzied wiggling and awkward attempts to flap his wings startled Emma. She squealed and her grip loosened.

The bird slipped from her hands in slow motion. She watched in horror as he struggled to right himself in mid-air, but his wings weren't functioning. His instincts couldn't compensate for his injuries. He hit the desk with a solid smack. The bird lay completely still, its tiny body contorted into a sort of macabre hokey-pokey pose.

"Oh my God. I've killed him," wailed Emma. "No, no, no, please."

"Emma," Jillian said reassuringly, "he's probably just stunned. Let's try to get him in the box."

Emma held the box open and started sliding it toward the injured bird, but when the box threw its first hint of shadow over the terrified plover, he attempted to scoot away. His good wing flapped and his uninjured leg paddled madly in a frantic attempt to escape. Emma slowly chased the flopping bird around the desk with the box. His feet scrabbled to and fro with a scratchy noise that was agonizing. Jillian cupped her hands behind the terrified bird and corralled him into the cardboard. Finally, with the lid in place, both Emma and Jillian plopped down in chairs—exhausted, but relieved.

Emma answered her ringing phone and listened to the caller. "So how long before you get here?"

"What is it?" asked Jillian.

"It's the volunteer. He said they're running behind. A call came in for a poisoned eagle, and they have to handle that before they head over. It's going to be a couple of hours. I don't know if I can bear him suffering for that long."

The Labor Day festivities had begun, and the Sea Sprite was filled with cheerful faces. But Emma found it difficult to divide her attention between interacting with the other guests and checking on the little plover. While she was downstairs chomping on a hamburger, she worried about the bird upstairs. She snuck a couple of grapes from the fruit salad, thinking they might provide energy and hydration. But when she removed the top of the box, the poor bird was curled up in the corner and wasn't moving.

"It's all right, Petey," Emma said. "I've got some grapes for you. You'll like these, I promise."

Emma squeezed the grapes and smushed them on the saucer she had borrowed from the kitchen. She set the dish of crushed grapes next to his little head, but the bird didn't acknowledge it with so much as a glance. Emma sat back dejectedly on the floor and watched the little bird.

"When will they get here?" she questioned, not expecting an answer. She placed the top back on the box and went back downstairs.

"Jillian, would you happen to have one of those flavor injectors for meat? Or maybe a small baster? I'm thinking I should try to give the poor little guy some water."

Jillian pointed toward a drawer in the island and told Emma to help herself. Rummaging in the drawer, Emma found exactly what she was looking for—a small eyedropper. She grabbed it and filled a red party cup with water. *I'm coming, Petey.*

Emma removed the top of the box and reached in with the dropper full of water. Petey didn't move. She tried to lift his beak with her finger and when his head was lifted, she squeezed the dropper to let some water out. She should have tested it on a paper towel first. Her overenthusiastic squeeze covered the poor bird's head and completely soaked him. He shook his head to disperse the water and then glanced at her through his tiny lids and wet feathers.

"Oh, God," she whined. "I'm so sorry. I'm making it worse. What am I supposed to do?"

Emma's cellphone gave her the answer she was looking for. The call was from Greg, the wildlife rehabilitator. Contacted as an alternate volunteer, he was on his way to pick up her bird.

"In the meantime," Greg said, "leave the bird alone and completely quiet in the box. Don't try to feed him or give him water. Shock is what kills most of these fellas. He'll get plenty to eat and drink when he's stable."

"OK, I won't try to give him anything," said Emma. "Well, anything else."

At five o'clock, Emma heard gravel popping in the driveway. She peered out her window and saw the huge, white Ford truck growl past the house and make its way to the rear of the property. Emma didn't waste any time. She rushed down the main stairs, through the hallway, and out the back door.

"Hi. Are you Greg?" Emma asked, flushed and out of breath. Greg exited the truck, accompanied by two women.

"Yep," he answered, "I'm Greg." He waved his hand to indicate the women and said, "This is Daisy and Pam. They volunteer at Beach Bird Rescue with me. We were together when we got the call and thought we would swing over to see what you've got."

Greg had a wide, pleasant smile. Genuine. His truck, the faded khakis, and threadbare plaid shirt made Emma think of hunters, not rescue volunteers.

"Thank you so much for doing this. Petey ... err ... the bird is inside."

"Petey?" asked Greg. "I like it."

"Yes, I figured he must be a boy, since I don't usually get along well with women—well, at least the women I work with." Emma looked apologetically at Daisy and Pam.

"No need to explain. I totally get it," said Pam. "I don't like most women myself. Too much drama."

Emma smiled and breathed a little sigh. The four of

them entered the house together, with Emma leading the way. Both women started firing off questions.

"What time did you box him up?"

"Did you move him?"

"Have you disturbed him?"

Emma answered honestly, worried she had done it all wrong. She replayed the injury, the transport, the box mishap, and her lame attempts to feed and water the poor bird.

"Don't worry," said Daisy as they climbed the stairs to Emma's room. You tried your best and that's what counts. A bird needed your help and you stepped up. Most people don't spend the time to pay attention. You may have saved one of Delaware's most endangered birds. You should feel proud."

"She's right," Greg added. "Most people just write a $25.00 check to the Humane Society and figure they've done their good deed for the year. Soon as the check's in the mail, they forget about it until they claim it on their taxes."

Emma opened the box.

"It's a plover, all right," said Greg, examining the bird. "Likely a fractured wing and leg."

"Sounds pretty bad," said Emma.

"There'll be a difficult period for Petey, but we'll do our best. You did the right thing by calling us. By the way, I'd place bets your bird is a girl."

"Thanks. I do feel good about helping him ... err ... her. Her life depended on me, I guess. But now, if anything bad happens, I'll feel terrible."

Pam jumped in, "Oh, sweetie, she's in great hands now. Our team has released several plovers after rehab. We'll do our best to get Petey, or Penelope, back on the beach as soon as we can."

"Penelope. I like it. That's great." A shy smile played at Emma's lips as she realized she was feeling a bit of a bond with the three of them. She walked them back downstairs.

"Want some food before you leave?" asked Jillian, catching them when they reached the reception area.

"I *am* kinda hungry," said Daisy, looking at Greg.

"Well, it will have to be fast. We need to get this little guy into a more controlled setting."

"There's still some barbecue left," said Jillian.

"Sounds good," said Greg, who had paused to look at the items in the display case. "Hey, that's a really nice harmonica. I actually play."

"Really? Would you like to take a look at it?" Jillian snuck behind the display case, removed the harmonica, and handed it to Greg.

"Wow, this is really sweet. She's a late 1930s Hohner. See these tiny letters here?" He pointed to a "C" and "G" stamped on opposite sides. "This means it plays in the keys of C & G. Nice box, too. Surprised it still looks that great. They were made special for the Germans."

"Thank you for telling me," said Jillian. "These things are all from a box that was found in this house during renovations. I've been trying to find out who owned it and how it got here, but I'm not having much luck."

Emma thought about the list in her journal. *Maybe this was her chance to help someone,* she thought.

Emma pulled Jillian aside and said, "We could work on your mystery this week during computer time. I'll bet we can uncover a few details."

"Oh, that would be great. Do you really think we can

find something?"

"I'm counting on it," said Emma.

Seated in the garden, the volunteers told the other guests about Emma's actions. Emma knew she had done just about everything wrong during the rescue, but the way they told the story made her sound like the star of the show.

"When I pick up a bird, I feel like a savior rescuing the world," said Greg, as if reading her thoughts. "I know it's total exaggeration, but it seems like we are keeping the species alive when a bird is saved. I get to be a hero, one bird at a time. Now you know what that feels like. It's pretty intense."

After being filled with barbecue, the trio loaded into the truck with the bird to head back to the rescue facility. Greg rolled down his window and said, "No act of kindness is ever wasted, Emma. I just wanted you to know. Thanks for doing this. Come by anytime to check up on Penelope."

She smiled and nodded as she watched them pull away.

Emma thought about the rescue all night. The next morning, she called Greg.

"Well, if it isn't the plover police," Greg said as he laughed. "How are you doing, Emma?"

"I'm great, Greg, how about yourself?"

"Well, I'm great, too, but I'll bet you didn't call to find out about me, right? So your bird is doing pretty well. The leg needed a splint and the wing was a fracture, not a break, which is good."

"Oh, that's wonderful news," Emma said, embarrassed by her relief.

"Matter of fact, can you hear all the fussing in the background? It's Daisy and Pam trying to get me to hand over the phone so they can talk to you. I'll let them say hello, too, but just wanted to tell you thanks one more time. You are kind to help out—it shows what you're made of. You should be real proud."

"Thanks, Greg."

"OK, OK, I'll give it to you. Just let me say good-bye to her. Emma, you still there? I've gotta say good-bye now and hand you over." Emma heard the shuffle for the phone and spent the next few minutes chatting with Daisy and Pam.

When she told Jillian about the enthusiastic call, Emma couldn't contain her joy. She thanked Jillian again for helping her rescue effort and for putting up with her non-stop talk about the bird.

"Know what I think, Emma?" Jillian asked. "I think you should stop in to visit while you're down here. I mean, you did just get off the phone with them and they are all there. I think it would be good for you. Matter of fact, you are so enthusiastic about bird rescue, maybe it's something you could volunteer for at home."

Emma pondered the suggestion. "You know what? You're right. That's a great idea." She pulled the Sea Sprite journal out of her purse and flipped it open to the list of goals she had started.

1. Make new friends
2. Help someone with a special need
3. Identify an interest
4. Get healthy

She was well on the road to making new friends, and she already found a new interest she could pursue at home. *Might as well put the rest of this plan into action.*

"First," she said, "I have a few things I'd rather do before I visit them. What do you say we have our first computer lesson?"

By the end of the afternoon, Emma had taught Jillian the basics of Pinterest and helped her post the Sea Sprite on a travel website. She felt great about helping out, but with the phone ringing and Jillian attending to the guests' needs, they hadn't spent much time on solving the mystery.

Before she crawled into bed, Emma opened the journal again. She had already decided to visit Petey/Penelope and look into volunteering closer to home. As for getting healthy and going to a gym? Well, she concluded that could wait. Helping someone with a special need? She was ready to get started. Her pen jumped into action, and it didn't take long for Emma to fill a new page in the journal with ideas focused on helping Jillian solve her mystery.

Over the next few days, Emma was rarely at the Sea Sprite. She visited the Rehoboth Beach Museum, Sussex County Recorder of Deeds, Rehoboth Beach Library, and even the public archives in Dover. For days, Emma had been returning to the Sea Sprite exhausted, but not today. Today was different.

Whoosh. She pushed the front door open. Jillian looked up over the top of her desk.

"I've got news." Emma struggled to catch her breath. "I found it. I mean ... I found some answers ... about the box."

Jillian stood. "Why don't you sit a minute. Breathe. Take your time."

Emma tried to be compliant. She plopped down with a sigh.

"What I'm trying to say is, I think I've found the owner of the box. Well, at least the people who owned the house when the box was hidden. Here, take a look."

Emma spread the contents of a folder on the table. "I've been doing some research. Look. Donald and Esther McGarry bought the house in 1924 for $1,275."

Jillian pulled her readers down over her nose and squinted her eyes to read the fine print. "Wait, could that be Reverend McGarry? He's the one with Helen in the picture I found at the church."

"This says the property sold in 1945 for $5,100 to George and Rebecca Wilson."

Jillian looked up at Emma. "George and Rebecca Wilson. My grandparents."

"The ladies at the Rehoboth Beach Library helped me access an ancestry database, and I pulled up some information there, too."

Emma reached into her bag, and with great pleasure, she handed Jillian another folder of paper.

Nervously shuffling them, Jillian began reading: " 'Helen, the daughter of Reverend and Mrs. McGarry, was born in 1927.' That would make her what, eighty-eight? 'Married Joseph Andrew Newell in 1944. Daughter, Virginia Jo.' " Jillian's voice dropped to a whisper. "Joseph Newell—J.N.— those are the initials on the harmonica." Her eyes shot open, and full of wonder, she said, "Virginia Jo. It can't be." Jillian's eyebrows were scrunched together in deep concentration.

Emma laughed. "It can't be what?"

"Amy's mom is Virginia Jo—she runs Ginny Jo's Bakery. And her grandma goes by Hellie, at least that's what I've always called her. Hellie? Helen. Ginny Jo? Virginia Jo. Our Helen has to be Amy's grandma, right?"

"Maybe you were closer to solving this than you thought," said Emma.

"So Amy's grandmother once lived in the Sea Sprite?

"Well, long before it was the Sea Sprite, but yes, it sure looks that way."

"Then the box may have belonged to Amy's Grandma Hellie. Wow. I would never have found this information without you. Thank you so much." Jillian grabbed her in a tight hug. Emma remained rigid for the first few moments and then relaxed—just a little—into the embrace.

Emma slowly extricated herself, a bit uncomfortable with the physical attention but pleased to have helped.

The following morning, as she prepared for the trip home, Emma arranged her snacks in the car. She was disappointed her vacation was over, but she made a reservation for next year and made Jillian promise to update her on the mystery box. Driving home, she reflected on how much she learned in one week. There were still things she wanted to improve in her life, but she was happy. The changes she'd made weren't nearly as difficult as she had imagined. *Well, at least most of the changes weren't difficult,* she thought. Grimacing, she reached for the baby carrots on the seat next to her.

Jillian's Journal

September 8th

The summer season ended on such a high note. Meeting Emma was a treat. I'll be the first to admit, before she arrived, I had already made up my mind. I thought it was going to be a difficult weekend, but Emma was a joy. She and that little bird. It reminded me I need to take time to nurture others. I've been so focused on rebuilding my life, but I may have some catching up to do. In fact, when I'm done here, I'm heading over to pick up Amy and Greta for Gramps' birthday party. Barb is coming, too.

My takeaways:

Our first summer is over. Funny, I never paused to think about what I'll do when I don't have any guests here. When I see an opening in the schedule, I'll fill it with some new energy and see what kind of trouble I can get into. Maegan will be home soon, so I want to leave lots of time open for us.

The Box – Emma found the missing pieces to this puzzle. What would I have done without Todd telling me about Helen's picture and Emma doing all the research? I could be wrong on this, but I've always called Amy's grandma "Grandma Hellie." How many Helens with a daughter named Virginia Jo can there be? Why would she leave these treasures behind? I can't wait to ask Amy about this—everything is lining up.

THE BOX GOES HOME

It's going to be a great day, thought Jillian. She was on her way to pick up Amy and Greta for Gramps' birthday party. Electricity shot up her arms, and goose bumps prickled through her skin. The thought of talking to Amy about her Grandma Hellie pumped a surge of adrenaline through her. She felt a teeny bit guilty that her excitement wasn't about the party, but she couldn't help herself. Turning up the radio, she pressed the gas pedal closer to the floor. She couldn't wait to get to Ginny Jo's Bakery.

After Emma left, Jillian had studied the paperwork until she thought her eyeballs would bleed. Amy's grandmother had to be Helen. There was no way another local family would have names matching so closely. Jillian thought about Amy's family history and tried to come up with alternative explanations. So far, she couldn't find any that were likely.

Jillian knew Amy's grandparents had opened the bakery in the 1950s and named it in honor of their daughter. When her husband died, Grandma Hellie put her soul into keeping their dream alive and in tip-top shape. Ginny Jo's Bakery soon became a popular fixture in Rehoboth Beach.

When Jillian was a child, Gramps would take her on Sunday afternoons to meet her friend at Ginny Jo's. She always ordered her favorite doughnut: the raspberry jelly. The first bite was a teaser. Sinking her teeth in, she would pull sweet dough into her mouth and tongue-test it for raspberry. Filling never showed up in the first bite. But the second bite? Jelly everywhere—all over the corners of her mouth, a big glob on the napkin, and fingers covered in sticky sweetness. Gramps started calling her "Jelly Girl," and the nickname stuck for life.

Mama Ginny was Amy's mom, but she made it clear Jilly was her daughter, too, just as much as any flesh she had given birth to. Her dedication coaxed Jillian through many dark, sorrowful days after her parents died. At times, the honorary status worked out great for Jilly. Most days, though, it meant she had to work, like Amy, to earn her doughnuts. Dishwashing, mopping the floor, making the coffee. Ginny Jo had a knack for keeping the girls occupied and out of trouble. Fortunately for all, they loved being together, and time in the bakery was considered a treat.

Many of Jilly's treasured childhood memories were made at the bakery. Walking in, even today, she knew her body would be enveloped in a warm, moist blanket of sweet air. The scent wrapped her in calm like a favorite blanket and drained the nervous energy away. Breathing in deeply through her nose was the best part. She could almost taste every flavor in the case, as well as the dough, the chocolate, and the coffee. Jillian still showed up at the bakery on Sundays to help clean ... and to get her raspberry jelly doughnut.

⚷

Just as predicted, the moment Jillian stepped into Ginny Jo's Bakery, her mouth started to water.

"Hey, you guys ready?" she called out.

"Yup, just let me rinse out this cloth. Help yourself," said Amy.

Jillian laughed as she took her first bite of the jelly doughnut she had already snatched on her way back. "After all these years, you think you need to remind me to help myself?"

"Good point. What's mine is yours, and what's yours is yours, right?" Amy snickered at her own joke.

"Hey, got a question for you. Is Mama Ginny's real name 'Ginny Jo'?"

"Nope. Her first name is Virginia, for the state she was born in. Her middle name is Jo, after my Grandpa Joe. Why?"

Jillian opened her purse and reached in slowly, removing the photograph of the young couple on the beach. "Is this Grandma Hellie?"

"That's her—a stunner, wasn't she? Where in the world did you find that?"

"It was in the box under the floorboards. It's the puzzle I've been trying to solve."

"Holy shit! Greta, come here." Amy was so loud and abrupt that Greta came running in. "Sorry, didn't mean to startle you. Look at this. It was in Jilly's mystery box." Amy paused and turned to Jillian, "What would this be doing in the box you found?"

"I'm not—"

"It's Grandma Hellie, and he must be Grandpa Joe." Amy jabbed her finger excitedly at the picture of the glamourous dark-haired beauty and her beau on the beach. "Look how happy they were."

Well, hello Helen. So the box *had* belonged to Amy's grandmother. Even though Jillian had suspected as much, she had to take a moment. All this time, and the answer was hiding in plain sight. Tears welled up. Jillian had no idea she had become so emotionally invested in the outcome of solving the mystery. She jumped up, the stool jolting from under her. Ignoring it, she said, "I want to take the box to her. Now. Right away. I need to get it to her."

"Whoa, whoa, whoa, sister. We can't just rush over there," Amy said.

"Amy, she's like a hundred years old or something. We need to take it to her, now," begged Jillian.

"Are you forgetting Gramps' birthday party? We can't skip it. I didn't make all these crazy arrangements for nothing. We can take it to her in the morning. Greta and I will go with you."

⚷

Gramps was all settled into his new digs at the nursing home. With Amy's help, his birthday party was organized and the fun was ready to begin. It was their tradition each year to try to come up with something crazier than the year before. So far, the winner of the craziest birthday party was his sixty-fifth, when they had hired the juggling clowns and belly dancers. Gramps always pretended to be shocked, but the truth was, he loved the commotion.

Jillian had called in advance and explained the unconventional plans to the staff at the nursing home. Instead of dissuading her, they joined in the fun by wheeling Gramps away under the guise of a therapy session, while the girls snuck in to decorate his room. Streamers, balloons, plates, and hats were strewn through the room haphazardly. His cake sat on the windowsill sporting candles "9" and "2" on top. His lamps were covered in silly string, his closet filled with balloons, and they had used erasable markers to write 'Happy Birthday' all over his windows.

Jillian tried to stay focused on the party. She was taping balloons to the door when a crown of pink hair snuck under her and walked into Gramps' room.

"Hi girls," Barb said. "I figured you were probably coming early, so I brought down some homemade coffee cake to celebrate Georgie's birthday. It's his favorite, you know."

"Wow, that's so nice of you," said Jillian. She noted the familiar use of a nickname. *Barb sure seemed to be keeping pretty close tabs on him.* It made Jillian smile.

Barb walked straight over and cozied up to Amy. "Now, honey," she said, "we both know where this coffee cake came from—and it sure as hell wasn't my mixing bowl—but that's a secret between us girls, right?" Barb added a wink to seal the deal.

"Absolutely!" agreed Amy, returning the conspiratorial wink.

"Great. Now that we have that out of the way, what can I do to help?" Barb clasped her hands together. "I love parties!"

"Here you go," said Greta. "Start filling up his bathroom with these balloons. That'll get him."

"Hurry," said Amy. "I think I hear him coming."

It was easy to hear Gramps being wheeled back to the room, as his voice always arrived before he did. "You know," he was saying to the nurse, "it's been years since a pretty thing like you grabbed my old bones like that. You're going to take care of me like that every day?"

"Yes, Mr. Whittaker. Every day."

"You sure I haven't died and made it to heaven?"

The nurse wheeled him into his room. Jillian broke into a chorus of "Happy Birthday," with Amy and Greta joining in. Barb headed straight for his wheelchair, planting a bright-pink Estee Lauder kiss on his lips. Gramps didn't even flinch. Instead, his eyebrows shot straight up and he smiled with enthusiasm. *Just as I suspected,* thought Jillian.

"Oh, my, my!" Gramps boomed. "All this fanfare, for

me?" He only showed a little surprise when the Hooters girls showed up with chicken wings, cleavage, and chilly backsides, making it the traditional birthday circus he thrived on each year.

As the party started to wind down, Gramps toasted his crew of ladies. "Thank you, girls. You've made this a very special day." His small crowd of fans whooped and hollered.

"Yes, thank you all. But, if you don't mind, I'd like to take a special moment to thank my Jilly." He sighed deeply, and the room quieted as he raised his plastic party cup. "I don't know how much life I have left, but I sure know I don't particularly want to spend the rest of it here. I want to thank her for working so hard to get me back home with the people I love. What you're doing means the world to me, Jilly, and I love you very much."

Jillian felt the sting of tears. She bit the inside of her cheek, trying to hold them back. Tasting the coppery bite of blood inside her mouth, she looked around the room and found she wasn't the only one with tears in her eyes.

"Here, here," someone yelled.

Jillian's chin quivered, and she swiped the salty tears from her cheek. "Gramps, I'll do whatever I can to get you home. I love you, too. All you have to do is heal up your right side so you can walk again, and I'll take care of the rest. We can't wait to have you home."

The party ended on a high note, with Maegan calling from Spain to wish Gramps a happy birthday. He must be on cloud nine with all the attention from this overly enthusiastic, all-female fan club. *No one deserved it more,* Jillian thought. Her cheeks were pink with happiness, and a sparkle of pride lit her eyes as she watched him bantering with her friends.

After the party, Jillian dropped Amy and Greta off at their

place with the promise to return in the morning. They would all go together to deliver Grandma Hellie's treasure box.

Back at the Sea Sprite, Jillian tried to squash her nervous energy, but didn't have much luck. She cleaned sporadically, took a long shower, and painted her nails. Still rattled, Jillian removed the ammo box from the display case. One by one, she took each item out of the case and carefully wrapped them back in the scarf. Nothing could take her mind off the anticipation of reuniting Helen with her memories. Much after her typical bedtime, she emptied a glass of wine and stifled a yawn. She decided sleeping was the fastest way to bring tomorrow. With that, she climbed into bed and fell fast asleep.

The next morning, Jillian had a hard time focusing on the drive over to pick up her friends. She was startled when the car behind her honked in displeasure, waiting for her to notice the light had turned green. At Amy's, she was still in a fog.

"Keys," said Amy.

"Keys? Keys for what?" said Jillian.

"Hand over the keys, sister. No way are you driving. You look like you're sleepwalking. Think I'm putting my fabulous life in your hands this morning? Not gonna happen."

Jillian begrudgingly tossed the keys to Amy.

In the back of her own car, Jillian was silently grateful. She could spend the drive thinking about what to say to Grandma Hellie. *This is going to be such a happy day for her. I bet she's wondered for years what happened to this box.*

After the doorbell chimed, all of them expected a long wait for the eighty-eight-year-old to get to the door. Helen surprised them when she immediately opened the door and greeted them with enthusiasm.

"Girls!" Helen reached for Amy first, wrapping her slender arms all the way around her and shaking until Amy's blonde hair tossed back and forth. Almost as quickly as she started, she dropped Amy and moved to Greta for the same greeting.

"Hellie!" Greta said. "So great to see you!"

"It's great to see you, too! Are you staying out of trouble?"

Jillian waited her turn in line, thankful for Helen's uplifting welcome. "Awww, sweetheart," Helen said to Jillian, "it's been so long! Come here and let me get some sugar. Amy said you're back in Rehoboth. Good for you. I know she's tickled to death to have you back." Helen pushed Jillian back at arm's length to get a good look at her. "You look just great. The beach must be agreeing with you!"

"Come in, come in!" She stepped back out of the way so the trio could pass.

No walker, no cane, no wheelchair. Jillian wasn't sure exactly what she had expected after so many years, but it certainly wasn't the ball of energy in front of her. Helen was dressed in a   seafoam-green cashmere sweater set that accentuated her gold eyes and stylish blonde bob. Her face showed plenty of wrinkles, but from Jillian's limited observation, they were all a direct result of her smiling so much. When she smiled, her face was vibrant.

"Are you girls hungry?" she asked. "I just finished breakfast downstairs, but I can call and order something up if you like."

"No, Grandma," said Amy, "we're good for now. We'll let you know if we need some, though."

"Good. Come on, come sit down with me. You haven't said a word about why you're here. It's so great to see you, but it's been at least three months. We can't go so long between visits anymore!"

"I wouldn't, Grandma," answered Amy, "but you're always going away to some exotic place. You don't sit still long enough for people to plan a visit."

Helen laughed, and the genuine sound tickled Jillian. "I suppose you're right, dear. I am pretty busy. I like it this way. Keeps me young … err … youngish."

Amy glanced at Jillian, giving her the signal to get started. Jillian shifted nervously, so Greta delivered the opener for her.

"Hellie, Jillian wanted to come over and give you some things she thinks might be yours."

"Oh? Did I leave something behind last visit?"

"No. No, these things weren't from your last visit," started Jillian. She crossed over and put the bag on the floor next to Helen. "These things were left a long time ago."

"Why I can't for the life of me think of what it might be."

Jillian reached down, lifted the green ammo box from the bag, and placed it on Helen's lap. "We renovated my grandfather's old house and my contractor, well, during construction, he stepped on a board in the bedroom and one end popped up. He took out the board and found this box under it."

Helen gazed at the box but made no move toward opening it.

"I've tried for months to figure out who it belonged to," Jillian continued. "Some people who stayed with me this summer knew what some of the things were, but it wasn't really coming together. Then Emma found the old property record at the library. It showed that your parents owned the house. Can you imagine how surprised we were? Then I showed Amy your picture. . . ."

"Grandma? Are you all right?" asked Amy.

Helen's face was transparent. There wasn't a smidge of color left in her cheeks. She sat staring at the box with her arthritic fingers wrapped tightly around it.

"Grandma?" Amy repeated.

Helen finally broke her silence. "Oh. Oh, my," she said softly, "I'm not sure. I don't know if ... if I should. . . ." Her eyes pleaded with Jillian. Sliding the box out of Helen's grip, Jillian opened the top.

"Shall we lay everything out here?" asked Jillian, pointing to the coffee table.

"No, dear. I don't think so. I'd rather not."

"You're right. It might scratch the table." Trying to help, Jillian reached into the box, pulling out the frayed piece of scarf that held the items close for so many years. She laid the scarf and its contents gently in Helen's lap.

A mewling noise escaped from Helen. She reached down to stroke the fabric. "He ... he took the other half. He was supposed to bring it back." Helen's voice was filled with anguish.

Too late, Jillian realized she had overstepped. "Oh, I'm so sorry. Here, I'll put it back." Jillian's hand reached out to retrieve the scarf bundle, but Helen quickly gathered it in her hands and caressed it.

Jillian, Greta, and Amy sat in silence. Their eyes darted back and forth, silently asking each other, *what should we say*?

"Grandma," Amy said, "you don't have to look at these things if it's painful. We thought you would enjoy them. Are you all right?"

"Yes, dear, I'm all right. It's going to take me a little time. I never thought I would see these things again." She fiddled with the scarf for several moments before speaking. "I gave him half of this scarf to protect him during his missions. He was supposed to bring it back, but he never did. After months passed, I finally gave up."

"I can put this away for you until another time if you'd rather," said Jillian.

"It's all right, Jilly. Why don't you show me the rest."

Cautiously, Jillian reached into the scarf and lifted out the silver locket. Helen gasped and reached for it. Pulling it close to her chest, she held it there, her eyes shut. Jillian and Amy looked at each other with worry when they noticed the tears sneaking out from Helen's lashes.

For a few moments, Helen's chin trembled. Then her eyes opened and she whispered, "His hair is in the locket. I can feel him." She sniffed and cleared her throat.

Forcing a weak smile, Helen reached into the scarf and pulled out the vial of sand. Wiping some stray tears away, her smile deepened. "Oh my. I remember the night I gathered this sand; it was a very special night." She laughed softly.

"Uh oh, Grandma, maybe you shouldn't tell us about that. Might be a little too much information." Amy's comment broke the mood and they laughed.

"No need to worry. I've never told anyone about it, and I'm not going to start now." Helen looked as though she were replaying the memory in her head.

"There should be some movie tickets in here, too," she said. Jillian reached in, pulled the torn movie stubs out, and handed them over.

"Ah, yes. *Casablanca*."

"I knew that one," said Jilly. "One of my guests told me what the tickets were. When did you see it?"

"We went to see it on opening night at the Blue Hen Theatre. Would you believe our tickets were twenty-five cents each? Oh yes, and after the movie, we went to Snyder's for a chocolate milkshake. All the kids in town hung out there." Her eyes were now as bright as her smile, and the girls felt the mood of the room lighten.

Next to come out of the box was the harmonica. Helen entertained the girls with stories of how he would play it. She put the instrument to her mouth and gave it a try, then laughed at the ruckus it made. "We used to have bonfires and marshmallow roasts on the beach. People always came up and asked him to play. I'll tell you, when he put it to his mouth, people would clap and cheer at the end of every tune."

Eagerly, Amy asked, "What else is in there?" Jillian pulled out the tiny metal purse and Helen laughed. She held it up for them to see.

"In my house, we weren't allowed to play any games. No cards, no board games, and no dice. It was considered a sin. According to my father, idle hands were the devil's workshop. So I would sneak out and meet up with friends to play board games. He always gave me the purse because he knew how much I liked it. After playing Monopoly with some out-of-towners one night, he snuck this into my pocket. He told me to keep it close because it was my lucky charm. I believed him and wore it on a silver chain."

Jillian piped up, "Oh my God, is that the cutest story ever?"

Amy nodded.

Reaching in, Helen pulled out the lipstick and the USO pin. "Ah ha! I've been wondering all these years where that lipstick went. I didn't remember putting it in there. Red lipstick was all the rage. One night at the USO dance, the lead singer caught me staring at her. I told her how pretty her lipstick was. She took me back to the dressing room, sat me down, and painted my lips. Then she told me to keep it. I was on cloud nine, and my girlfriends were green with envy. I wore it the night I met him; that's the same night I got this pin."

"This is so great. Did they have bands there, Hellie?" asked Greta.

"Did they have bands? Oh goodness, yes. Most of the time they were local bands, but once in a while, they would hire out. In fact, Merv Griffin—*the* Merv Griffin—was in a band and came down to play at some dance. I can't recall which one; it might have been the Lifeguard Ball."

"Who's Merv Griffin?" asked Greta.

"Don't tell her. She doesn't deserve to know," teased Amy.

"Was this the same lipstick you were wearing in this photo?" Jillian slowly pulled out the photo and handed it to Grandma Hellie.

Helen stared at the photo for several minutes and nodded her head. After studying each detail carefully, she pressed it against her heart and began to sob. Every heart in the room broke for Helen. No one knew what was causing her pain. Was it the loss of her youth? The death of Grandpa Joe? The memory of their happiness? It may have been a little of each. But to hear her reminisce about the love of her life—then witness her despair in the purest form—was heart wrenching. Jillian blinked her eyes quickly to hold the tears in and felt a strangled noise building in her throat. She looked across the room. Greta sniffled, wiped her eyes, and turned away. Only Amy was strong enough to speak.

"Grandma," said Amy, "I know you miss him, but he's

here right now, with us. I think Grandpa Joe wanted Jilly to find these things and bring them back to you. Look at the picture. See how in love you two were? That kind of love lasts through eternity. You were both so lucky to have each other."

Helen gently smiled at Amy. She set the photograph down on the table and surrounded it with the other memories. She wiped the tears from her eyes again and leaned back into the couch.

"Thank you. Thank you all for bringing this to me. You have no idea how much this means. I'm just so thankful."

Jillian sighed with relief.

"I'd love to hear more about you and Grandpa Joe back in the day." Amy smiled brightly, trying her best to shift the mood again.

"It's a little bit complicated, sunshine girl."

"It's OK. You don't have to talk about it."

"It's just ... the man in the photograph ... isn't your Grandpa Joe." She paused and let it soak in before she continued.

"I promise I will tell you all about it soon, but first I need to talk to Ginny. You've brought me a great gift, and I'd like to treasure it alone for a bit."

"What do you mean it isn't Grandpa? Those are his initials on the harmonica and on the back of the picture. I don't understand."

Helen sighed. "The man in the photo is a different Joe. I knew him as Joseph. He was a B-24 pilot during the war, and I met him on Rehoboth Beach in 1943. It sure didn't take him long to sweep me off my feet. I was in love and felt like a princess. My parents would never have approved. That's why I had to sneak out to see him. When Joseph flew out in August for his last mission, I gave him half of my scarf as his lucky charm. I waited for months, but heard nothing. One May morning, a soldier came to tell me Joseph wasn't coming home. The soldier was your Grandpa Joe."

"Wow, so that's how you met Grandpa?" asked Amy.

"Yes. They served together and grew to be best friends. Your grandpa told me he fell in love with me before we ever met. He said he heard so much about me, he felt he already knew me. When Joseph died, your grandpa was with him. Joseph made him promise to find me and tell me how much I was loved. So he did."

"Why did you hide everything in the box?"

"My parents would never dream of letting me go on a date—or even hang out with a boy. So each time I brought home a special trinket, I had to squirrel it away with the rest of them so my parents wouldn't suspect what I was up to."

"But what about the initials on the harmonica and the photo? Those are Grandpa's?"

Helen smiled. " 'J.N.' are Grandpa's initials, too, but the initials on the harmonica and on the photo were those of his best friend and my first love, Joseph Natale."

"That explains so much," said Jillian. "I'm so sorry for your loss."

"Things always turn out the way they are supposed to, dear. I married Grandpa Joe, and we had a wonderful life together. I've always been grateful he found me."

"Grandma, why does Mom need to be here? You never told her about dating the pilot? Does she know you used to live in Jilly's house?"

"Please, sweetheart. I promise I'll call your mom in the

morning. For now, though, I'd rather you not share this with her. Everything is fine. It's just wonderful you found this and brought it to me. But if you girls don't mind, I'm pretty tired. I think I'd like to rest now."

"Take all the time you need, Grandma. This must be overwhelming. We can talk when you're ready," said Amy.

"Thanks. I just need to rest a bit. Think you girls can show yourselves out?"

As the girls filed out in silence, Helen placed the items back into the ammo box and closed it on the coffee table. Her hand remained resting on its top.

⚷

Jillian stood alone in the yard observing the Sea Sprite. She could hardly believe it had been less than a year since she had returned to live here. Pleased, she noted the attention to detail its exterior now boasted. Shiny, white columns now stood proudly supporting the verandah roof. Colorful gingerbread trim topped shiny windows.

The key warmed her hand. Standing on the familiar porch—surrounded by glossy paint and the sweetness of her successes—Jillian gave the key a solid push into the gleaming brass lock. She lifted the doorknob up and to the left. The door swung open, welcoming Jillian home.

Large swaths of light reached through the windows to rest upon the gleaming floors and warm the room. She looked across the quiet space and studied the display cabinet. It was empty, its mystery solved. Jillian smiled. She would find her own treasures to fill it again.

And so it goes, she thought. *Without an end, there could be no beginning.*

Jillian's Journal

September 12th

Unbelievable. Yesterday, Grandma Hellie shared the story of the box with us, but it turns out there was more to the story. Mama Ginny's father was the pilot, but he was killed in action before he knew she was on the way. Grandpa Joe tracked Grandma Hellie down and found her, pregnant with his best friend's baby. He married her, and the two raised Ginny Jo together as their daughter.

Of course, they forgave Grandma Hellie—it's easy to see that she just wanted to protect her daughter, but my heart is breaking for Mama Ginny. She never even had the chance to get to know her biological father. Amy said they are going to try to find some of their relatives, see what they can learn about the family. I can't imagine not knowing where you came from or what your true background is. I kind of know the feeling, but at least I knew both my parents. I'm so grateful for Gramps.

Gramps was in the war, too. I have to remember to ask him about his experiences. The nurses told me it should only be a couple more weeks and he can come home. I'm so excited. I'm hoping he gets to come home the same time Maegan does. I'm going to throw one hell of a party, and this one will top them all.

Time to start planning a new year. Our little sea sprite made sure this year was perfect. I can't wait to see what next season has in store for us.

QUESTIONS FOR DISCUSSION

1. *The Sea Sprite Inn* opens and closes with an intriguing statement that lays out one of the major themes of the book. "Without an end, there can be no beginning." What do you think this means? Share some examples where you noted an "end" that was followed by a "beginning".

2. Early in the story line, Jillian was more terrified of staying in her current situation than she was of failing on the way to something new. Is it better to take a risk and fail than never try at all? Would you consider adopting a project like *The Sea Sprite Inn* under similar circumstances?

3. Brad found the World War II ammo box under the floor during renovations. What was the role of the treasure box in the story line? Why do you believe finding its owner was so important to Jillian?

4. Carol always seemed to be in a hurry, but patience has its own reward. Can you relate to Carol's need for speed?

5. Beating the UVA women's swimming record was Maddie's goal. Do you think she was so focused on the record that she suffered as a result, or was her focus commendable?

6. Little Chloe had some difficulty communicating. Do you think Beth and Steve had the same challenge?

7. Callie found a very special swimsuit that may have had unusual qualities. Why did her attitude change when she put it on?

8. How did Samantha, Kate, and Regina handle the competitive environment differently? Do you think jealousy emboldened their actions?

9. Things aren't always what they seem to be. Brody and Karen both discovered this in different ways. Why do you think Karen didn't believe Brody loved her? Did Brody allow

his imagination to get the best of him in the lighthouse?

10. Relating to women had been difficult, but when Emma focused on helping others, fun, friendly interactions seemed to happen naturally. What are some suggestions that could help Emma build new friendships when she returns home?

11. Gramps told Jillian, "You need to decide what kind of future you want and who you want to be. Then do it. Simple as that. Do yourself a favor; don't make it any more complicated." Can people determine their futures by deciding what they want and doing it? Describe some examples of complicating a simple goal.

12. How does *The Sea Sprite Inn* figure as a character in the story? Could you picture it clearly? What was your favorite spot?

13. It's time to confess. Did you get choked up when Helen told her story? Shed a few tears for Marjorie? Did your jaw clench or your hands sweat when Mack shared the history of the lighthouse? Cheer for Maddie to swim faster? Which scenes were the most poignant? The most dramatic? What will you remember most about *The Sea Sprite Inn*?

14. What message stayed with you long after you finished the book?

WARNING – THE FOLLOWING QUESTIONS CONTAIN SPOILERS

SPOILER ALERT – If Marjorie had gone to breakfast with John, would you have been disappointed? How would the story have changed if only one of them, or both of them, had gone to the meeting place?

SPOILER ALERT – How did **you** feel when Helen was looking at the treasure box? What do you think went through Helen's mind when Jillian showed her the box?

SPOILER ALERT – Do you think Ginny Jo had a right to know who her real father was? Would you have made the same choices Helen did? Are secrets inherently wrong, or sometimes justifiable?

THE END ...

Because without it, there would be no beginning.

Did you enjoy *The Sea Sprite Inn*? If so, please post an online review, tell your friends, and visit www.catandmousepress.com for more great books.

Follow Lynnette on Twitter: @LynnetteAdair, and Facebook: www.facebook.com/LynnetteKAdair.

CPSIA information can be obtained at www.ICGtesting.com
Printed in the USA
BVOW08s2336170716

455776BV00001B/1/P